The dynamics of fighting for animal rights is nothing new, but the way attention is being given to it is being taken up by some unlikely sources. A new children's book series by a former professional of the United Nations going by the pen name of K. F. Kristi has been released for the main purpose of bringing the rights of animals to the attention of children and parents alike.

R. F. Kristi, the author of the Inca book series lives in France. She holds a doctorate in economic development and has travelled and lived in many countries around the world. She is fluent in English and French.

With a deep commitment to animal rescue efforts, Kristi has a keen interest and love for animals. She created the Inca Cat Series for younger readers, up to age 8 or 12 and also animal lovers.

Read more about R.F. Kristi and the Inca Book Series at *www.incabookseries.com.*

R.F. Kristi

THE CATS WHO CROSSED OVER FROM PARIS

Inca Book Series: Volume One

AUSTIN MACAULEY PUBLISHERS™

LONDON • CAMBRIDGE • NEW YORK • SHARJAH

A CIP catalogue record for this title is available from the British Library.

ISBN 9781787108745 (Paperback)
ISBN 9781787108738 (E-Book)

www.austinmacauley.com

First Published (2018)
Austin Macauley Publishers Ltd.
25 Canada Square
Canary Wharf
London
E14 5LQ

Acknowledgments

Illustrations by Natalia Yamokova and Assad

Contents

Inca, a Siberian puss, tells the story about her furry family – her brother Fromage, who is addicted to cheese and considers himself a cheese monger, and her sister, Cara, a gorgeous but timid Siamese. Inca, an avid fan of Dr. House, considers herself the leader of the troupe and responsible for the well-being of the family. They own, according to Inca, Missy, a young humanoid who has a well-established cheese shop in Paris. The story revolves around how Missy decides to move to London with her co-partners, Jacques and Genevieve, to run their new cheese shop and café. Can Fromage leave his pal, Charlotte, behind? Soon after arriving in London, the three cats accompany Missy to their neighbor's house where they meet Monk, a blue Russian cat and Terrance, a golden retriever owned by their famous neighbor, a detective named Solo, living in the same compound in Kensington.

Things start to get interesting when Monk tries to help their neighbor, Polo, a sad little Pekinese whose mistress, a formerly well-known opera singer who is pining for her lost husband, has her valuable diamond necklace stolen. Can Inca and her family assist Monk and Terrance to recover the diamond necklace and resolve Polo's problems?

With thanks to my editor Kwame Boafo

Chapter 1

We are moving?

Major changes in life occur when you least expect them. It all started one sunny and glorious morning in our chic but compact apartment in the 7th district of Paris. The sky was blue and our comfortable apartment, which overlooks the river Seine, was basking in the white clouds. This first day in the month of June was bright and twinkling, and in thousands of apartments across Paris the warmth of the June sun refused to budge, making the temperature as hot as a fully heated baking oven.

The fur balls in our apartment were in their seventh heaven with pleasure at the warmth of the sun. *Quel Bonheur!*

I was, as usual, sitting on the back of the sofa of Missy with one paw delicately poised and hanging down to her shoulder while she served croissants, baguettes, cheese and tea to our visitors. Missy had laid out a splendid spread for our guests on the small round dining table; an enticing brunch.

The scenario never changed whenever we had guests. Missy was her usual chatty and hospitable self while I took a backseat, beautifully poised with the posture I maintain for the customary compliments on my looks. My brother, Fromage, was eagerly eyeing the breakfast tray full of goodies and wondering if he would get a morsel of cheese from Missy. Cara, my sister, was lying on her back at Missy's feet, gently touching her with her paws trying to get the attention that usually comes my way!

Oh well! All was as it normally is in the Missy and puss household!

My ears pricked up as Missy started telling the guests, her good friends Genevieve, Jacques and a strange man I had never met before that she addressed as Monsieur Chevalier, that "No, we will not be taking all the furniture but a few nice pieces that I have collected in Paris. We will be moving to a furnished cottage."

My ears twitched in the direction of Missy as I moved from an elegant lounging position to sitting up with wide-eyed attention. I sat up and listened with interest, pretending to be absorbed by the flowers on the ivory-gray Persian rug on the polished parquet floors while they continued their discussion. By putting two and two together, I managed to get the whole story more or less correct. 'Quoi' we were moving? What was going on? Alarm bells started ringing in my head!

This was news to me and I thought it was best to read the mail on Missy's table to get more information before alerting the others. There were letters and pictures she had been so engrossed in after coming in from work ignoring "Dr. House" on the box, the television series the household concentrated on most evenings. "Dr. House" is my favorite television series, the one I watch with avid interest while we lounge around in the evening after Missy gets home from work.

Missy's friends and Monsieur Chevalier left after enjoying their brunch and talking about the move. Monsieur Chevalier promised to get back with a quotation very soon. After they had left, Missy planted a kiss on my head, eyed Fromage and told him, "No more cheese, young man!" She gave a tickle to Cara and ran for the door, saying "I will see you gals in the evening; Inca, you are in charge until I get back." Missy has a habit of calling Cara and me 'gals' and so Fromage has got in to the habit of calling us 'gals' too.

I took a leisurely walk to the dining table, making sure not to look agitated, and took a peek at the letter lying on top. Yep, we were indeed moving! It was a letter from Missy's aunt in London, Aunt Florence. Missy had decided to move to London. Since I was well aware that Missy would never leave us behind, we were moving as well.

There were several photos of Aunt Florence's residence in London from various angles. There were different rooms and corners of her charming cottage that I decided to concentrate on later, after I had alerted the others.

I said to Fromage and Cara, "Stop fidgeting and get over here, I have news for you. We are moving! We are leaving Paris!"

As I anticipated, they stopped in their tracks and raced towards me, skidding on the polished parquet floor and stumbling over each other.

'*QUOI?*' said Fromage with an alarmed look on his face, his whiskers twitching. "Leaving Paris, but I can't do that. I am a true Puurrrisian, what about my French cheese? What about my visits to my cheese shop on Avenue de la Bourdonnais?" he cried, tapping his beret in place; an automatic reaction that I had noted whenever he gets excited.

His cheese shop....? Honestly, I thought. Missy, Genevieve and Jacques own a small but fabulous little cheese shop on Avenue de la Bourdonnais in the 7th district of Paris, not far from our apartment. They bought the shop from Monsieur Lepayre when he retired.

It is true, Fromage was actually born in the cellar of that shop before the owner, Monsieur Lepayre, sold it and moved to the countryside with Fromage's mum and dad. It is also true that Fromage visits his old home often with Missy, perched on the cat carriage of her bicycle. He sometimes spends the whole day in the shop where he has his paraphernalia set up in the basement, his birthplace. He wonders around the shop happily, examining the new cheeses and inhaling the aromas of the different types of French cheese. He also enjoys getting titbits from Genevieve, who could never resist his longing, large brown eyes.

Missy and Fromage - Off to the cheese shop

Monsieur Lepayre's cheese shop was reputed to be one of the finest in Paris. Monsieur Lepayre had available a wide and varied selection of French cheeses. Giving recommendations on the type of cheese to have with lunch or dinner was his specialty and Jacques, when he became co-owner of the shop, had every intention of carrying on this tradition. Customers would spend their time selecting their cheese and there was never any hurry once they entered the shop. Fromage would listen and learn from Monsieur Lepayre, as had his dad and mom. The scent of cheese and the atmosphere added to the reputation of the shop that Fromage considered his own enterprise.

Cara looked bewildered. "Mummy.... I mean Missy," said Cara with an apologetic look at me. "Missy is coming too, right? You know I cannot leave her behind, Inca. I never could, though you have explained to me several times that as a Siamese Seal Point, with my ancestry from the royal palaces of Thailand, I should behave more like a noble cat.'

I sighed; one would think that I would leave Missy behind for a minute. The problem with Cara is that she came home to us, meaning Missy and I, when she was just two months old. She considers Missy to be her Mum and could not sleep without Missy snuggling up to her in bed from day one of her arrival. I have patiently tried to explain to her that, while we all adore and love Missy, as superior cat people we must never be too obvious in our affections for humans. But I suspect my advice somehow doesn't get through to her - somewhat like pouring water on a duck's back.

I took a deep breath and started explaining the news from what Missy had said and her correspondence with Aunt Florence. You remember Aunt Florence, right? Here is what she says in her recent letter to Missy:

"Missy, dearest, I have found the perfect house for you and the little ones – my own. The moment you said that you would be moving to London I thought it was time to put my plans into action. Your Uncle Norman left this house to you in his will. I have been living here after he passed away but now it's time to move back to Provence. I miss my old home and France. I have looked after your house for five years like my own, but it is time to return it to you, *ma Chérie*. The different levels of the house with the enclosed and protected back garden would be ideal for the pets. I will leave most of the furniture behind as my home in Provence still has my beautiful vintage furniture. You will love it; it has some lovely old pieces of furniture that will go well with the antique pieces you have collected in France. I will, of course, come at least twice a year to visit you and my little Inca, Cara and Fromage.'

She went on in this enthusiastic vein for the rest of the letter, not giving any thought to how our hearts were pounding. Yes, our hearts were pounding like a well-oiled mechanical bunny rabbit beating his battery operated drum, 'Boom! Boom! Boom!' at the thought of leaving our beautiful apartment in Paris. We had lived here most of our young lives, with the exception of Fromage who joined us when he was eight months old. Don't get me wrong, I love Aunt Florence who has been very kind to Missy over the years. She was married to Missy's uncle, her mum's brother, Uncle Norman. She was originally from Provence and is a lovely French lady, with very kind eyes.

Fromage was getting more and more agitated at the thought of leaving behind his much loved cheese. Cara had tears in her blue eyes, and her little black and brown nose was shaking with concern that we were to be transported to this new place leaving Missy behind. That thought brought back memories long forgotten of how frightened she was of being packed in a box and transported in a car away from her parents and five siblings, until she saw Missy's smiling face and myself ready to kiss her all over and welcome her to her new home.

At that time, Missy was of the opinion that it was lonesome for me to be without a companion, especially when she had to leave for work. What she didn't know was that, when she was not at home, I had the habit of sneaking out to the rooftop of our building where I had met Labelle, a grand dame of a puss, mature in years. She was beautiful, astute and wise, and had immediately taken a fancy to me and become my good friend and mentor. Labelle is of the Chartreux breed with a sweet and quiet disposition. She is currently the vice-president of the Cat Council of the 7th district and she persuaded me to start attending the monthly meetings of the Council as a fully-fledged member.

Missy, not knowing all of the above but believing in Hemingway's philosophy that "one cat just leads to another," had bought Cara from a family of Siamese breeders living in Chartres. Chartres is a historical village that is famous for its beautiful old Cathedral. I loved Cara the moment I saw her, even though she was a tiny little tot, mewing pitifully. My friendly licks soon calmed her down; I remember licking her all over, making her my sister.

Cara is quite grown up now and looks gorgeous. However, because of her shy nature, her beauty does not stand out as it should. She is a Seal Point with a close fitting, short-haired coat which is glossy and sleek. She has complementary color patterns, dark brown, nearly black, points on the mask of her face, ears, legs, feet and tail but the rest of her body ranges from dark to light beige in color. Missy had bought her a blue shawl that matches her blue eyes which she wears tossed around her neck as I do with mine, which is burgundy pink. We have wool shawls in winter and soft silk shawls in summer when the weather gets warmer. *Très chic, non?*

Missy has a funny story that she tells about Cara's long, slender tail which is permanently pointed up with a slight curve. According to Missy, Cara's ancestors were made responsible for the princesses of Siam's precious rings. These rings were slipped onto the tails of the Siamese cats. To avoid the rings slipping off the tails, the Siamese developed the famous curve in their tails. True or not, I believe Cara comes from a noble lineage. If only I don't have to keep reminding her to stop slouching and walk around more like me, confident and gracious despite my small stature. Definitely not like Fromage who romps around and falls over his own feet in his haste to get somewhere, anywhere at all.

Missy and I were both expecting some trouble from Cara. Her breed has a reputation for their audible and expressive meows and Siamese cats are supposed to have a lot to say about everything. But we were pleasantly surprised. Cara has a very soft and gentle meow that is rarely heard. She is shy and withdrawn and rarely causes any disturbance in the apartment. She is still babyish in her ways and always needs to cuddle either with Missy, or with me. In the mornings when Missy is away, she comes and sleeps on top of me wherever I am, smothering me like a soft heavy blanket. Given that she has increased in weight and grown rather long, the experience is not all that comfortable but I tolerate it all the same as she is my baby sister.

Fromage joined us sometime later, when Missy met him at the cheese shop that was subsequently bought by Missy, Jacques and Genevieve. The owners were retiring to the South of France after managing their successful cheese shop for decades and found it difficult to take all the cats with them. As they could only take Fromage's mum and dad with them, they wished to find homes for Fromage and his brother. Missy could not resist agreeing to give Fromage a home, his brother had already been taken by a regular customer of Monsieur Lepayre.

Cara cuddling up to me in our younger days

Fromage is a handful; gauche and talkative with a vivid imagination. He sports a light black and brown striped coat of his own natural fur, he is high spirited and is always ready for an adventure of any type. He is also somewhat of a clown and has a clumsy side to his nature. I cannot count the number of occasions when Fromage has misjudged his target when leaping onto some place or other, more often than not resulting in a sorry tumble. Despite Missy's constant yells of, "Fromage watch out!" he merely looks at her as if to say, "*Moi*? Surely you don't blame me for the broken dish on the floor." Though exasperated, Missy would look at Fromage, the disarray that he had caused, and would quote Lenny Rubenstein saying, "Even if you have just destroyed a Ming vase, just purr, and all will be forgiven." She would then start laughing while picking up naughty Fromage and caressing him. I have not met this Lenny character, but he sure knows what he is talking about.

We try to avoid the delicate subject of Fromage's pedigree. No one knows exactly what sort of cat Fromage is. When he came to live with us, Missy assured us that he is of impeccable character. In her own words, "Fromage is a rare, rough diamond and with the help of you 'gals' we will soon polish him up to become invaluable." We soon became very attached to him and his infectious optimism, though I am the first to admit that he does have a tendency to get us into trouble. All the same we find him quite adorable.

Though Fromage, Cara and I are not blood siblings in the cat sense, we have pledged to be one family, owning Missy together. Of course Missy is of the opinion that she owns us, as humans tend to think. We leave her to relish this misguided conception and the liberty to say so. Imagine us cats having a mistress or master ? *Jamais de la vie !* This may work for dogs, but not with us cats who prefer to own our human companions. This is a silent covenant which humans do not fully understand, though the more intelligent of them are very much aware of this ownership dynamic between us cats and humans - sometimes even before they invite us to enter their homes and their lives.

Let me not bore you with details of my brother and sister. I got back to the conversation at hand as Cara turned her sky blue eyes to me, "Inca, you have to convince Mummy… I mean Missy to not send us away."

She made that request to me because both Fromage and Cara realized soon after their arrival that I have telepathic powers with humans, unlike them. Since birth, I have had the power to communicate telepathically with my former companion, Marie-France, and then with Missy when I came to live with her. That is, I am able to send information or messages directly from my mind and can receive information from another mind. Growing up, I slowly came to realize that I have mind-to-mind communication powers and the power to read another's mind.

Fromage in his element in 'HIS' cheese shop

Don't get me wrong, most animals understand what humans are saying. Cara and Fromage both understand what Missy says very well, if they care to pay attention as I generally do. When there are humans around, I generally concentrate on what is being said, unlike Cara and Fromage. I do this mainly because I am very inquisitive and like to know what is going on around me. Also, I take the role of '*Chef d'état*' of the kingdom of Missy very seriously. I need to know everything that is going on whether it is important or not. If someone comes to the apartment, I am the first at the door to introduce myself and find out why they have come and what they want, while Cara waits for me to give her the green light to come out. Fromage, of course, is in a world of his own, dreaming of his cheese shop and other cheese related ventures.

The issue is not for Cara and Fromage to understand what Missy is saying but to get Missy to understand what Cara and Fromage are saying. I do not have that problem since I can get my thoughts through to Missy's mind. A very useful talent, I may add. I have finely tuned the art of telepathic communication with Missy as I am around her all the time.

"Cara, I don't think Missy will stay behind and send us to London. In fact, Missy is going to London and I am sure she will take us with her."

"Are you sure, Inca?" came her prompt reply, already the fear subsiding in her eyes.

Fromage looked far from happy, fearing greatly of losing the smell and taste of his delicious French cheese in our cheese shop on Avenue de la Bourdonnais. I was also not happy about moving from Paris. What about our beautiful apartment overlooking the river Seine? What about Pierre, my personal coiffeur? Pierre singles me out amongst all his customers, praising my lovely smoky, gray and white color, and the way my tail falls like a handsome feather. He frequently tells Missy how well behaved I am compared to his other clients. What about Chantelle, our yoga teacher, who visits us each week to do yoga with Missy and Cara? What about Franck and Yvette, the young couple from Madagascar, who come in to clean our apartment? Not to mention René, our next door neighbor's young son, who babysits us when Missy travels on business. They are all my friends and admirers, and fuss over me every time we meet. I would miss them all terribly.

I crouched down on the table to read Aunt Florence's letter once again more carefully and take a look at the photographs. I was determined to see what was roaming around Missy's mind that evening…well at least after the Dr. House program was over, as I couldn't possibly miss that. I pride myself as a feline version of Dr. House, intelligent, observant and out of the ordinary though I was not sure if the rest of the household had this perception of me. I constantly dream of being like Dr. House, solving cases and saving lives. Well no one could contest the fact that I am intelligent and observant with a serious countenance. I rarely see Dr. House smiling, and I try to imitate that look. He is my hero.

The photos on the table were quite nice. The garden looked promising; we had never actually enjoyed the delights of a garden – as we are apartment felines.

"Who is that on the adjoining fence?" said Fromage who was peaking over my shoulder. "Looks like one of our kind." How could I have missed him? Yes, right on the divide between the cottage and a larger imposing house posed a very distinguished looking individual, gazing right into the camera, as if it was important that he gave his large, sharp eyes to the photographer. Am I mistaken? It was a handsome Russian Blue, with long slim legs and large golden-green eyes. He was a large cat, though a bit portly around the waist.

"Even overweight cats by instinct know the cardinal rule: when fat, arrange yourself in slim poses," as John Weitz, the successful German menswear designer, is supposed to have advised. Monk knew how to pose, alright. Compared to Cara, Fromage and me he was very large indeed, but his size masked his rotund waistline. It is believed that such breeds are descendants from the royal felines owned by Russian Czars.

As you may have noted by now, I am from the domestic cat species: A *Felis silvestris catus* or more commonly called a *Felis Catus*. I am of the Siberian race also known as the Moscow Semi-Longhair, and my ancestors come from Russia. We are known for our agile jumping skills. Although Siberians are known to be large, I am a pocket-sized version weighing just three kilos. I have short strong hindquarters, large well rounded paws and a magnificent tail. My coat is silky, smoky grey and white. Siberians moult once or twice a year, but Missy found this fabulous coiffeur named Pierre who attends to my hair regularly. He shampoos and trims my hair and nails, so I never really have very long hair.

I wish to mention that my breed is well known worldwide. Several of my Siberian folks are well known personalities. 'Dorofei', a Siberian cousin, owned the current Russian Prime Minister before his untimely passing. Former Soviet president Mikhail Gorbachev was owned by another Siberian relative. Missy has even shown me a photo of a famous kin of mine being admired by President Obama and the First Lady of the USA. As you can see, we are a breed that moves in the highest echelons of society.

Very curious and interesting! "I wonder who this Blue Russian is," I thought to myself.

I took a more careful look at Aunt Florence's letter. She talks of a Monsieur Monk residing with the world famous Detective Solo, who could be a good influence on 'our friends'. Meaning us. How could she say that? Yes, for sure he did look handsome and intelligent. But that means nothing. He could have a sour character and be more like Ivan the terrible inside his shiny coat, unlike me in the genre of Dr. House without a walking stick.

Cara leaned over Fromage to take a look. "Hmm… very good looking, though not as elegant as you, Inca," said Cara, giving my face a lick. "Nor as cute as you either, Fromage," she added with another lick to Fromage.

Fromage looked interested. I know, though he doesn't actually voice it, that he feels slightly dominated by the three females that he shares his abode with and secretly yearns for the company of the male species. I notice how he sucks up to Jacques, even though it is Genevieve who drops morsels of cheese at him. Some of these morsels he stows away in the basement of the shop where his stuff is.

"Let's not worry ourselves about this now, you two," I said. "Let me see what is going on in Missy's mind this evening when she comes home." Saying so, I padded away to have a snack. With all the excitement I felt rather famished.

That evening after dinner, I sat on Missy's lap while she was examining Aunt Florence's letter and photographs. I wriggled to a sitting position and looked deep into her eyes, conveying all our fears to her mind.

At this point, let me enlighten you about Missy. I consider Missy a livewire, full of energy and goodwill. She has a heart of gold. She has golden brown curls, a heart shaped face and bright brown eyes. Nature indeed had done a good job putting our Missy together. She is very sportive and generally walks around briskly in a bouncy manner. She is slender, alert and is quite tomboyish. She loves the open air and walking in the fresh outdoors; you would find her every morning composing her trim body in contorted yoga poses which Cara likes to imitate. Her main appealing character, in my opinion, is that she adores cats, especially the three of us. To us, Missy is a vibrant, loving 30-something that is our most cherished possession.

Missy is half American from her father's side and British from her mum's side. Unfortunately, we never had a chance to meet her parents as Missy lost them when she was very young in an airplane crash. She was at a young age when she came under the guardianship of her maternal uncle, Uncle Norman. Uncle Norman was married to Aunt Florence who came from the Provence District of France. Although Missy had attended university in America, at the *alma mater* of her parents, she was very much French, owing to Aunt Florence's influence. At the moment, Missy's only living relative is Aunt Florence.

According to Aunt Florence, Missy developed her love of cats at a wee age to counter the loss of her parents; she had been presented with an orange colored kitten that she immediately christened 'Minou'. There is, in our study, a large photo of Minou in the arms of a very young Missy, next to our own group photo taken more recently. Minou, after a full and happy life, passed away at the age of 21 years and Missy still has not forgotten her. Missy spent her formative years in Provence with Aunt Florence and Uncle Norman. They moved back to London later when Uncle Norman's own father passed away and left him the cottage.

Missy spends a lot of time playing with us, particularly with Cara who, although just over one-year-old, still behaves like a little baby when Missy is around. To Cara, Missy is her mum and she is Missy's baby. Let me give you a typical example; Cara has always been attached to this little cloth snake that was named Monsieur Hizz by Missy when it was given to Cara as a welcome home present. To this day, Cara carries around Monsieur Hizz in her mouth. Wherever Monsieur Hizz is the night before, in the morning Cara makes it a point to place it on Missy's bed as a wake up gift. This has been going on for quite some time and I am wondering when Cara will outgrow this habit. Of course, she is aware that this action alone earns her numerous brownie points from Missy in the form of cuddles and kisses.

Yoga session with Cara and Missy

28

In addition to being an avid cat lover, Missy is what you would call a smart business woman with an MBA under her belt. She works for a consulting firm and helps small to medium start-up companies of exclusive luxury lines to expand, mainly in Europe. While doing this for some time, she also ventured into the French cheese shop business, the one she bought with Jacques and Genevieve, her two partners, from Fromage's mum's guardian, Monsieur Lepayre. Fromage's mum owned Monsieur Lepayre and still does, and they now live in Normandy together with Fromage's dad and Monsieur Lepayre's wife, Simone.

Cara and I were never really that fond of cheese until Fromage joined us. Fromage's conversation mainly revolves around French cheese, so whether we like it or not, we have become very familiar with the different types and kinds of French cheese.

Those who sell cheese are sometimes talked about as cheese mongers. Many cheese mongers are experts in cheese such as, for example, Jacques our good friend. However, the term "cheese monger" does not specifically refer to a cheese expert. *Affineurs* are those who age cheese. The two titles are not mutually exclusive. Some *affineurs* may also be cheese mongers and vice versa, but that is not always the case.

One could say that Jacques was both a cheese monger and an affineur, like our Fromage. Someone who knows a lot about cheese, though, is simply a cheese expert like his wife Genevieve. Fromage, as mentioned earlier, has the habit of hiding cheese in the basement to age the morsels he collects. Hence he considers himself a cheese monger and a cheese affineur.

Missy is neither; she is just a good business person. She started out by helping Jacques and Genevieve when they first bought their business, even though you cannot classify a cheese shop, even in the élite 7th district of Paris, as a luxury line. On the way, she also became a part-owner of the shop, having invested with the young couple, fifty-fifty.

I looked deep into Missy's eyes, and she looked deep into mine, murmuring *'Inca, Inca'* and showering my head with kisses.

Having conveyed my fears and those of the others about this impending move to unknown London, I cuddled on her lap.

After a few moments of reading her book, Missy walked over to the sofa where Fromage and Cara were tussling, with me in her arms, and put her arms around us. It had worked. My thought process is amazing!

"Inca, Cara, Fromage...we are moving to London! Jacques, Genevieve and I are opening a second cheese shop in that city. We will be fine in London. You remember Aunt Florence, no? The one who brings you many treats when she visits from London and spoils Inca rotten? Well, she is moving back to Provence and returning the cottage Uncle Norman left to me in Kensington."

Missy continued, "It is a very comfortable cottage with an enclosed private garden at the back. The cottage is situated adjacent to the main house within the same compound, both properties surrounded by all types of foliage; trees, bushes and flowers, and enclosed at the back and sides with a high wall to keep us safe. The great-grandson of Monsieur Solo is the current owner of the main house."

"Monsieur Solo is a well-known detective. He owns Monk whom I am sure you will like very much." I muttered, "You mean Monk owns him." She went on, "Monk is used to visiting Aunt Florence at the cottage, so you will have to be welcoming to him. Though the cottage is within the perimeters of the main house and its garden, we will be very independent. Aunt Florence has told me that Monk is affectionate, intelligent and courageous. Hobbs, Monsieur Solo's chief servant and assistant, lives in the basement of the main house with his dog, Terrance. But I understand that Terrance and Monk are great mates and Aunt Florence assures me that Terrance has abundant respect for cats."

"He better," I mumbled to the others, clenching my claws.

"It will be a big change for all of us, but I am confident you will be happy there," she stroked Cara saying. "We'll all be together, Cara, my precious. Fromage, you will be very important in

30

establishing the new cheese shop in London as we are proposing to specialize in French cheese, in which you are an expert. In fact, I have big plans for you, my little friend, as you will be our mascot. As for you Inca, you will love it in London and will be in charge of our little brood making sure all of us are fine."

It turned out that our cheese shop on Avenue de la Bourdonnais would continue to be owned by us. It was so successful that they had hired a manager and staff of two to keep things going in our absence. This eased Fromage's mind. He told us that we should all go to the shop before leaving and he would treat us to the different cheese he had aged, smacking his lips at the thought of tasting these aged morsels. I agreed, but to be honest I am not into cheese, French or otherwise. Cara likes it better, but I would make an effort to taste one or two of Fromage's hidden gems just to please him.

Missy went on to explain that she was not selling our apartment in Paris, but just leasing it for one year to a young American couple. I sighed with relief. At least our lovely apartment would not be lost forever. Fromage would have a new cheese shop to take care of, and Cara was content that we would all be together.

After all these reassurances, Fromage pulled his beret more firmly on his head and started whispering non-stop to us about his new cheese venture in London and all he would do to ensure that it was a roaring success. Cara was reassured that we would all be together and cuddled deeper into Missy's lap, licking her hand.

What about me? I loved Paris and our apartment. I loved watching the lights of the boats as they gently moved on the river Seine in the evenings and early nights. What about Pierre, my coiffeur? Would I find another like him in London? What about my other human friends?

Missy did not seem too concerned and I understand that, next to Paris, the Londoners loved their animal companion. Perhaps Missy would find someone to my taste over there. Above all, we would have our own garden and that of Monk. New friends to meet, new horizons to cross! Oh well, being the eternal optimist that I am, I decided to hold my judgment and to pad along to the kitchen to see what interesting delicacy Missy was laying out for us to overcome our distress. I had immense trust in Missy to ensure that all would be well and she depended on me to keep the troupe together.

I thought to myself that we had to attend the Cat Council to say goodbye to our Parisian cat friends before leaving Paris. Fromage had added thoughts. "It's only one month before we leave for London. Let's do something we have never done before," he said.

It suddenly struck me. *Why not let my siblings take a look at the Iron Lady dancing?* I myself had never seen her dancing in the night. I understood from Labelle, my friend and co-president of the Cat Council, that it was a sight to behold. The Iron Lady was supposed to be a terrific dancer. Looking at her dancing would not be difficult as she lived just next door to our own apartment building and we would have a clear view of her dancing if we were on our own rooftop at the precise moment she started dancing. I understood from Labelle that she danced only for about five minutes every night on the hour. This would be a great treat for all of us and something that Missy would not object to if she knew about it, or so I reasoned.

I brushed aside Fromage's other outlandish idea of taking a boat ride on the river Seine. This would mean actually crossing the highway in front of our building and meeting all the motor monsters roaming about on the highway. The distance was not far as the river Seine was across the street where we lived and we often watched the people getting on and off the boats that went up and done the river. But I had no faith in the motorized monsters as they could possibly run over one of us. The very thought of that gave me the jitters. I know that it would have been very hard to survive a run in with a speedy monster. We were used to moving about in Missy's monster; this was being inside the monster which was quite comfortable, but it was something else being knocked down by one of them.

That weekend, Missy took off to London with Jacques and Genevieve to finish certain work related to the new French Cheese Shop they would be opening soon. René came as usual to babysit us. But since he goes to university and has a part-time job in a restaurant, he only came in very early in the morning to feed us and clean our litter tray. He is a swell guy and it was nice that we would get to see him before our departure.

More importantly, we would be alone most of the time; that would give Fromage and I the opportunity to escape through the balcony and attend the monthly Cat Council of the 7th district to say '*adios*' to all our friends.

The Cat Council of the 7th district of Paris is made up of senior cats living in that district. Although I am not yet considered a senior, I have many friends on the Council and I am aware that my family is well known and much respected in this circle because of my connections in the group. It was Labelle, the Vice President, who had introduced me to the Council, after all.

Fromage wanted to pass by the shop on Avenue de la Bourdonnais to say goodbye to his good friend Charlotte, a little rodent who lived next door in the science lab, that had become friends with him since his early years living in the basement of the shop. It was on my mind to leave very early on Friday morning given our impending departure. Fromage was all for this idea. As you can imagine, Fromage has an audacious spirit that took in every opportunity out of the routine as a welcome challenge.

The thought of new adventures gave him a spring in his step and a gleam in his eyes. I wondered if it was a good idea to have suggested this outing to him. But if we didn't do this now, when would we? After all, we were leaving our beloved Paris and we had no idea when we would be back. Suddenly I too felt light in spirit, why not? It would be our last escapade in Paris until we came back, who knows when?

Chapter 2
Adios to old friends

The morning arrived with an excitement in the air which set us tingling. Rene's arrival had lost its usual charm and his friendly greeting was hardly acknowledged nor was the yummy food that he set out before us. He tried to get us to play, but our thoughts were on our impending getaway. We were impatient for him to leave. Even Cara, who was to stay at home, seemed to have caught the infection and bubbled with anticipation.

When we were about to leave after René had left, Cara had other ideas about our departure. She refused to be left behind all by herself, alone in the apartment. So knowing that the waterworks would start to flow if I refused and that I could never resist her teary large blue eyes, I agreed that she could join us, saying, "Hurry up, go and finish your breakfast; also drink some water as we will probably be back very late and may not have anything to eat or drink until we get back."

I had forgotten that Fromage had other plans. He wanted to finish off the morsels he was maturing in the basement of our Paris shop on the way to the Cat Council meeting. I just had a look at his gleaming eyes to realize the thought swirling in his head. For once I thought this was a good idea as I too didn't relish the idea of not having something to eat until late in the evening.

Before we set off, I sat down with Fromage and Cara to decide the itinerary and to offer advice that, if by any chance we were separated, that they should come directly back to the apartment instead of trying to find each other at the Cat Council or our cheese shop in Avenue de la Bourdonnais, or anywhere else. The route over the rooftops was relatively straightforward, uncomplicated and hardly posed much of a hazard. But given the responsibility I felt for my younger siblings, I had a natural tendency to be cautious.

When I move out of the apartment to go anywhere without Missy, which is not often, I always go via the rooftops of Paris as much as possible. I mainly just leave the apartment to attend the monthly Cat Council meetings, if they are being held when she was not at home. Thereby, I avoid the busy roads and heavy traffic with the great and small motor monsters of all sizes and shapes whizzing past as if hurtling to catch a departing train.

Our building is situated on a busy highway just next to the grand Iron Lady, the famous Eiffel Tower. I was familiar with the rooftops in this area. Our apartment building was one of the first buildings at the top of the street facing the river Seine on the corner of Avenue de la Bourdonnais. Our cheese shop was further down the avenue and I was in the habit of taking this route, jumping from rooftop to rooftop until I got to the building where our cheese store was located on the ground floor.

Missy was not aware of these sojourns and neither would she have approved them. The thought of us roaming the rooftops of Paris without a chaperone would have given her the shivers. Missy has a tendency to be very protective of us. In fact, Missy is far too protective of us, in my opinion.

The plan was to go directly via the rooftops to our cheese shop and through the courtyard at the back of the shop, then enter the High School and visit Charlotte in the science lab. We planned to spend time with her and then invite her to the basement to finish off the morsels tucked away by Fromage to ripen. Fromage could then quietly say goodbye to the shop that we would not be visiting again and we would go to the Cat Council meeting on the rooftop of the High School in the afternoon before dropping off Charlotte in her home on the way back. It was important for us to say adios to Charlotte. There was a strong link between Charlotte and our family. We were all fond of her but she was Fromage's special friend.

The Cat Council of the 7th district of Paris takes place once every month on the rooftop of the building housing the High School where Charlotte resides. Charlotte's hamster cage was located in the science lab of the High School on the basement of the building. During the summer holidays, these Council meetings are held at noon but when school is in session, the Council generally meets after school hours later, around 5pm Fromage's encounter with Charlotte went back to the time when Fromage's mum and dad left the cheese shop after the original owner sold it to Missy, Genevieve and Jacques.

Many folks visiting our cheese shop on Avenue de la Bourdonnais had always expressed interest in Fromage as he was often in the cheese shop looking very busy. He watched with avid interest when the cheese was being sliced and wrapped. He sometimes trotted around with the customers as if asking them to try one or two of the cheeses he recommends. Many customers, on meeting Fromage, were curious about him. Questions posed by customers related to – *What is his name? Why was he named Fromage? Does he live in the shop?* Fromage has a tendency to make an impression on the people who meet him. When Missy took over the joint ownership of the cheese shop with Jacques and Genevieve, she had agreed to take over the young cat left behind by the former owners since she did not wish it to be sent to a rescue home. However, given his attachment to the shop, it was decided that the move to Missy's apartment would be gradual.

Missy was very serious about abiding by the strict rules of hygiene that should be maintained in food stores in Europe. She had made it a point to follow a training course on such rules and had also learned to handle food products. She was an expert on product labeling, respect of temperatures of food products, disinfection of premises and a whole ream of other regulations.

Jacques has the same certification, but has a completely different perspective on health regulations from that of Missy. Nevertheless, Jacques had to pander to Missy's dictations on hygiene regulations when Missy became a co-owner of the shop.

Despite all the precautions and thoroughness regarding hygiene, one morning a small rodent named Charlotte sneaked into the basement of the French cheese shop on Avenue de la Bourdonnais. She was as flexible as a rubber band. She had run on top of a pipe connecting the building where she resided and that of the shop, and slipped under the rail of the ventilator in the basement into the cheese shop. It was the strong aroma of the French cheese that had tempted Charlotte from her environment.

It happened one hot summer afternoon. It was almost one o'clock in the afternoon, the sun was shining brightly and the general mood was one of laziness. Everyone was out to lunch, and Charlotte was on the lookout for a more substantial lunch than what the guardian of the High School usually fed her in her cage which consisted of two or three pieces of lettuce, a piece of old apple, half a tomato that had seen better days and a piece of stale bread.

She left her small cage and slipped through a half open window tempted by the odor of juicy, melting cheese bubbling in the basement next door waiting to be poured into little cartons. The wonderful smell was too hard for her to resist. Charlotte was not on her first trip outside her home environment, though it was the first visit to the shop. She had learned the art of opening the door of her cage venturing out and returning when she felt tired.

Despite her young age, this little rodent had foiled vicious rat traps placed everywhere by unfriendly people of the two-legged human form. Charlotte preferred a fair fight, even if it was with a broom of a janitor or a hysterical housewife. On such occasions, she behaved liked a proud bull dodging a taunting bullfighter in the arena. Many ignorant people often mistook her for a small mouse. Fromage, whose home was then in the basement of the cheese shop, had been observing the juicy, melting cheese in a great big urn in the basement when he saw Charlotte enter. While Charlotte was dreaming of fresh bread and cheese, Fromage thought that perhaps he had discovered a new friend. He was rather lonely and sad as his little brother, mum and dad had moved away a week ago.

In his excitement to reach Charlotte and introduce himself as a playmate, and in his hurry to jump to the ledge on which Charlotte was observing the room, Fromage upset some plates with a loud clang and plunged into the large pot of melting cheese just below where Charlotte was sitting. As he slowly descended to the bottom of the pot, he watched the stacks of cheese balls with amazement, carefully arranged on their shelves, staring at him motionless. Nothing came to disturb the cheese surface from regaining its density and natural thickness, no bubbles, no wrinkles, no dull cry, nothing. From the beam, Charlotte had witnessed the whole scene and memorized every detail. She froze like a statue but that did not prevent her from nibbling on the piece of cheese into which she had just plunged her little paw. The thought flashed in her mind; if only she could have one of those smartphones that unobtrusively moved under desks from the hand of one student to another, particularly during biology exams, she would have filmed the scene and would have spread it around the neighborhood. The news would then spread like a shock wave! Throughout the city she would become the new heroine, David had defeated the hairy fur ball of a Goliath.

She could then begin a new life and live like a Pasha, pardon the pun, 'Pamster'. Unable to realize her dream, she was content with helping herself to the largest piece of cheese she could possibly carry and she returned quietly to her 'lab pal' in the classroom.

The scene did not go totally unnoticed, however. Indeed, for the good luck of Fromage, it came to be viewed in full on a small screen upstairs in the shop. Jacques and Genevieve, hearing the clatter, had looked immediately at the screens transmitting what went on upstairs and in the basement of the shop. They had seen the astonished young cat slowly sinking into the cheese pot.

Jacques moved with lightning speed. Very quickly, his large arm plunged almost entirely into the large pot and pulled out the young cat by his tail making him let out a loud yowl. The kitten shook his head to remove the cheese that was embedded in his fur and had covered his eyes.

From that moment onwards, Jacques and Genevieve christened him 'Fromage'. His passion for cheese originated from that incident, as if his baptism by cheese had established his future as a cheese monger.

Missy was not satisfied with this name as she had discussed with Cara and me about the arrival of a new young cat and how we would name him "Marcel" after Marcel Proust, the famous French novelist, critic and essayist well known for his famous book titled *'In Search of Time Lost'*. But fate had intervened and the young cat was reborn as 'Fromage'. Once we got to know him better we all, including Missy, think that the name 'Fromage' just suits him fine. I often wonder why Missy thought of naming our Fromage, *Marcel.* Fromage is anything but an intellectual. Missy, despite all her practical business sense, is a dreamer and romantic. Fromage - a Marcel Proust? Is she dreaming or what?

After the incident, Charlotte visited the basement often. Fromage, in his delight at finding new company, always shared some of the morsels he had with Charlotte. To Charlotte's credit, she never stole any more cheese but only took what Fromage offered her. They used to spend long hours enjoying the morsels of cheese while Charlotte recounted the goings on of the mischievous students attending classes in the science lab. Fromage in turn spoke of his beloved cheese shop, and the different kinds of cheese in France. Fromage was aware that there were 350 to 450 varieties of French cheese grouped under eight categories, *'les huit familles de fromage'*. He found a good listener in Charlotte as she listened to him whilst nibbling on her cheese. As the friendship grew stronger, Fromage was surprised to find that his yearning and thoughts of his brother and parents grew less and less.

By that time, Charlotte was no stranger to Jacques, Genevieve and Missy. Since the shop is under television surveillance they soon found out about the friendship between Fromage and Charlotte. Missy told us about this strange friendship that had grown between them. The television screens in the shop were connected to Missy's laptop at home, hence we were able to observe our soon-to-be little brother, Fromage, and his friend Charlotte, with interest.

Cara and I followed our talkative new brother-to-be from the inside of our apartment. He had a habit of talking non-stop on the subject of cheese. We both found him quite an interesting character and were impatient to meet him physically, which we finally did when Missy brought him home. But she made it a point to take him back to the cheese shop often, in the basket attached to the front of her bicycle because I had told her how Fromage considered himself a cheese monger and how attached he was to the shop.

When Fromage came to live with us, he had no knowledge of the Cat Council or that they met next door to our cheese shop on Avenue de la Bourdonnais. When Cara had grown big enough I took her along to the Council so that the members could meet her. Many of the senior lady cats tickled and licked her to welcome her. I wished to do the same with Fromage as he was now our little brother and part of the family.

When Fromage was nine months old, Cara being nearly one-year-old and myself just nearing one-and-half-years-old, I decided to take not only Cara along for the Council meeting but also Fromage to introduce him officially to all present and establish his immediate membership in the Cat Council of the 7th district.

I remember that day very clearly. We entered the rooftop of the High School the easiest way - through the back of our cheese shop via the courtyard into the great hall of the High School and then up the deserted steps up to its rooftop. It was 4:30 p.m. Since the meeting was taking place when schools in France were in session, it was to start at 5pm, as school would have finished by 1pm. The students and teachers, as well as the caretaker, would have left the premises by that time.

The great black cat named Amador, who is our president and well known for his strength and cunning, was seated on the top of a ledge above more than fifty cats ranging from young to old of various colors and sizes. Amador examined his long, sharp claws. There was a mixed group of cats present, from street cats to cats living in comfortable homes, mostly apartments as there were very few individual houses in the 7th district.

Every cat on the rooftop was very much in awe of Amador. He had built his reputation over time and was famed for having fought with a particularly nasty dog in the neighborhood reputed for his hostility towards cats. The dog had at first tried to completely destroy Amador but he had not reckoned with Amador's courage.

Amador had come back to fight the dog again and set him running for his life after ripping his ear to shreds with a strong blow. We heard that Amador's reputation had spread amongst the canine world very fast.

Amador did not live in an apartment but on the rooftop of a restaurant in the 7th district. He was a loner but commanded respect the moment he entered a room or opened his mouth. His purr was raspy and low, imposing immediate attention. Amador had been re-elected twice as President of the Cat Council of the 7th district. He was revered by both young and old of both male and female cats living in the district.

Our Cat Council was generally run by democratically elected members attending the meeting. However, our President has such a strong personality that he tended to command respect and be obeyed whenever he pronounced judgment. The only requirement was that a standing member had to introduce a new entrant wishing to attend. All issues concerning street and house cats were discussed by the Council, especially when there was an issue that would affect one or more cats living in our district.

Upon us pattering on to the rooftop where the Council met, Fromage and Cara stayed close by my side. Cara, even though she had visited with me a few times before, stuck to my side like glue, not budging an inch even to say 'hello' to the young ones her age. Fromage, his eye as wide as the saucers that Missy used to serve us our milk, studied everything and every cat; for once he was speechless and stayed by my side. He had absolutely no idea that the Cat Council met next door to his birth place. He wondered if his mum and dad had been members of the council and if anyone knew of them or would remember them.

It was quite a gathering. Several of the older cats studied the younger ones, whispering to each other about the younger ones while the younger cats tried to show themselves to the older cats in their best light. When I walked in with Cara and Fromage, I noticed we were looked at with curiosity and some elements of admiration. We were quite a handsome trio, well-groomed and thanks to Missy, perfectly coiffed and dressed. The appreciative glances of those present supported this assumption.

I slowly went around the rooftop introducing Fromage as the latest member and reminding them that Cara had been here before with me. There were purrs of welcome to my expanded family. We gradually arrived at the paws of Amador and Fromage gave a deep bow as was expected from a young newcomer to our esteemed leader. I had groomed Fromage well on what was expected of him as a first timer when he was brought before our leader. While introductions were being made, we heard a sudden commotion at the back and a sudden ominous silence on the rooftop.

Two guard cats, sturdy street cats and friends of our leader who were selected not only for their friendship with him but also for their powerful stature, cried, "Halt, who comes here?" Soon after, between them, they pushed a little creature of the rodent type to our leader Amador. Amador stopped his discussions with us and his matronly Vice-President Labelle, who had introduced me to the council and whom I consider my mentor and friend. He looked down with arrogance at the little intruder who had dared to enter a rooftop full of cats, disrupting the council meeting. The deadly silence erupted into a chorus of low mutterings and ferocious growls from the cats present.

Amador said, "Quiet everyone," and in his low growl snarled, "I want to know who this bold, insignificant pipsqueak is. Who dares to venture into our presence?" The little rodent seemed to suddenly realize amongst whom she was and shriveled into herself.

Fromage gasped and whispered to Cara and I, "That is *mon Amie,* Charlotte. She must have seen us passing by and came to be introduced to Cara and you as I have been speaking about my wonderful pretty two new sisters. Inca, she is my friend. We have to save her." I recognized the little urchin, who I had first noticed spending her afternoons with Fromage, on Missy's laptop.

Big Chief Amador: Judgement on Charlotte

I looked at Fromage's pleading eyes and, despite my uncertainty, I knew that I had to take charge of the situation immediately before an unpleasant and deadly crime was committed before our very eyes. Such a situation would have surely traumatized Fromage and Cara. We were one family after all and my siblings looked up to me as their leader and defender.

Despite my apprehension at addressing the gathering for the first time, I got up, took a deep breath and said as loudly as my voice would allow me, "Leader Amador, the wise and powerful, you know that if two members vouch for a stranger, he or she will be welcome to attend the council."

Labelle murmured, "Inca, I believe this rule refers to only cats." But I turned to her with pleading eyes and turning again to our leader said, "Esteemed leader, there is no specific mention of cats. Our rules say that if a stranger is vouched for by two regular members, that stranger is welcome to attend." Labelle nodded in agreement and smiled a gentle encouraging smile seeing my nervousness while Amador stroked his chin deep in thought.

Fromage jumped up and said eagerly, "I am Inca and Cara's new brother, Sir. The newest member of this gathering. I can vouch for this stranger." Cara, not to be outdone and ever ready to help us, jumped up next to Fromage and for once hiding her shyness, looked into Amador's eyes with her beautiful blue eyes and said, "I do too, Sir." I saw Amador getting lost in Cara's blue eyes and knew that he was smitten.

He dragged his eyes away from Cara and looked at me full in the face, his shrewd eyes meeting my large light green eyes. I quickly took this opportunity to send wave after wave of positive vibes forcing him to protect Charlotte and let her join the council. He shook his head as if not believing himself but said roughly and loudly, "Very well, I order the guards to hand over the stranger to the keeping of Inca and her family and the stranger can continue to stay on the roof for the duration of this meeting."

I gave a sigh of relief and Fromage quickly whisked Charlotte into his scarf making her disappear from sight for the rest of the meeting as if he didn't trust some of the burly cats who were eying Charlotte smacking their lips. There were low mutterings of, *"these uppity apartment cats and their ideas,"* from some of the street cats. Fromage knew that every cat was bound by the order of Amador, but we all knew too that the congregation, including my friend Labelle, was completely stunned by the ruling of Amador as he was known for his rigid judgments concerning the rodent species. It was a relief when the Council ended the session that day and we quickly moved out, not waiting to chit chat as we usually did, to our basement in the cheese shop to take a breather and think about the close encounter of Charlotte.

From that day onwards, Charlotte became our grateful and loyal friend. She was already very attached to Fromage, but she included Cara and me in the same category, and we in turn became attached to her. She turned out to be a clever and brave little hamster with a wicked sense of humor which she used liberally to keep us amused. So when Fromage said he wished to say goodbye to Charlotte, both Cara and I readily agreed as we had become attached to this rare specimen and our only hamster friend.

We carefully set out through our balcony onto the ledge leading up to the rooftop of our building, over the parapet and several other buildings until we reached the building of our cheese shop. I led the way making sure to go slowly. We cautiously came down to the back yard of our cheese shop and swiftly crossed over to the High School which was deserted, it being a sleepy Sunday afternoon.

We silently followed each other down to the science lab where Charlotte was busily doing her exercises running round and round her revolving cylinder-shaped cage, making quite a racket. She stopped in her tracks when she saw us come in and gave us a wide welcoming smile.

Charlotte said, "Wait a minute, let me open my cage and join you. What brings you this way? I am very happy to see you. I was wondering how to spend my Sunday afternoon."

She soon got out from her cage and hopped over to us. Fromage said, "Come on, Charlotte, I want you to join us in the basement and help us to finish the oldest and ripest morsels of cheese that I have been aging for months."

Charlotte jumped with joy, and replied, "How kind of you and what a great way to spend our Sunday afternoon - tasting aged cheese. I know that you are a very talented *affineur, mon Ami*, the aged morsels are sure to taste just fabulous."

We crept back in to the basement and Fromage soon dug out the morsels he had been aging and said, "What a wonderful feast." We all tucked in. Let me say again that I am not the most ardent cheese fan, but some of the aged morsels were very delicious and ripe. Fromage does have talent as a cheese *affineur*. After our feast we comfortably stretched out to listen to what Charlotte had been up to since we last met.

After some time, I reminded Fromage that it was time to break our news to Charlotte and say goodbye to the store; we also had to say our adios to our friends gathering at the Cat Council as we probably would not see them again, or at least not for a very long time. Who knows when we would be back in Paris?

Charlotte looked at Fromage with troubled eyes, "Are you going away, Fromage, *Mon Ami*?" Fromage suddenly looked very sad and I knew he could not say a word. So I tried to ease the situation for him by explaining to Charlotte how we had recently learned about Missy, Genevieve and Jacques opening a French cheese café and store in London, and that we had come to say adios to our friends before leaving.

"How could we not do this and just disappear like thieves into the night?" I said. We explained how upset we had been when we heard the news, but that Missy was our mum and we could not abandon her; we would go where she goes and it was the same for her, she could never leave us behind.

Poor Charlotte, she looked at us sadly and said, "I love you all like my own family. The family I never knew nor had. From the day the three of you saved me at that Cat Council, I vowed to myself that you are my family and I belong to you." We all looked at each other wretchedly and Fromage said, "Inca, could you please say adios on my behalf to our leader and friends. I will stay and try to comfort Charlotte. She is my oldest and best friend; she comforted me when I first lost my original family, and it is now my turn to comfort her. When you finish with the Council, pass by and pick me up."

Agreeing, Cara and I slowly trotted back with a heavy heart to the High School and climbed the stairs to the rooftop to say adios to our other friends. We knew what Fromage said was true. Charlotte was his friend even before he became part of our family.

Goodbyes are not something I relish. Adios always leave you disturbed and unhappy. Cara reminded me of the time she had to leave her original family behind. Although she was very happy with her new family, saying goodbye to loved ones is always an upsetting experience. I agreed. When Missy went off on her business trips, the experience was unsettling even though we knew very well that she would come back soon.

The spacious rooftop was already full when we got there. I went up to Amador and Labelle on the podium with Cara to whisper to them that we were leaving for London and if they could please make this announcement to our friends. Both Amador and Labelle seemed upset about our departure. Amador looked deep into my eyes as if trying to understand something that was puzzling him. I recalled the time I had telepathically convinced him to save Charlotte. He was not aware why he had turned into a softy, but he always looked at me as if he was trying to see what the connection was between us.

When Amador made the announcement, there was silence first and then everyone came around to lick us goodbye, asking about Fromage and expressing their regret at our departure. We told them about how sad Charlotte was and that he had stayed behind to console her but that he had sent his good wishes to all of them. They understood as they would never forget the time Charlotte attended the cat council.

After a lengthy goodbye session and speeches from some who had been close to us, we left our friends dejectedly to fetch Fromage. It was getting rather late and I had plans to surprise Fromage and Cara with the sight of the dancing Iron Lady in all her glory before heading back home for our Skype call with Missy later in the evening. Missy had a habit, wherever she was in the world, to make sure she Skyped us to say goodnight. If she was not at home, we felt some comfort seeing her familiar face on the screen of the laptop and hearing her voice asking us how we were and wishing us goodnight.

As we entered the basement we found a happy and excited Fromage. We were surprised because when we left we had seen two sad friends looking at each other mournfully as if their closest relative had passed away.

"What's up, Fromage," I said. "Are you ready to leave now? Have you said all your goodbyes to the shop and Charlotte? Where is she? I was hoping to say adios to her for the last time," I asked.

In response, Fromage leaped up and did a jig. "Gals, Charlotte is coming to London with us," he said.

"What?" I said. "I wonder how Missy is going to deal with this news." Just then Charlotte entered with all her worldly belongings packed in a miniscule backpack attached to her back. She seemed pleased and as excited as Fromage. "Let's go, friends," she said. "I have never seen the Iron Lady. This would be a wonderful sight to remember for life and to take away of our last memory of wonderful Paris." She climbed on to Fromage's neck and settled down comfortably inside his shawl, disappearing from view. I wondered how I was going to cope with this new development; hiding Charlotte from Missy, smuggling her to London and then convincing Missy to accept Charlotte as one of the family.

Cara turned her blue eyes to me and said, "Don't worry, Inca. Fromage and I will help you and we will convince Charlotte to be obedient and listen to you. She is a sweetheart in any case and it would have been too bad to leave her behind. After all, she does consider us family. So we have no choice."

"No choice indeed," murmured Charlotte's voice from within Fromage's shawl while he gave me a happy smile. There was no doubt about it. Fromage was over the moon carrying his little friend on his back. For him, the important part was that he was no longer miserable; he had his friend coming along with him. We would all be together.

When we slipped out of the basement of our shop it was close to 9pm. Labelle had informed me how the Iron Lady danced every hour for five full minutes starting every evening at nine. I had always wanted to see her dancing and thought it would be a breathtaking treat for the others.

We speedily trotted in a single file with me leading the way, Fromage behind me with Charlotte on his neck and Cara last in line. We arrived shortly on the roof of our building and perched together on the edge of the roof, observing the Iron Lady. She was an unusual beauty alright - a splendid specimen, very tall and upright. Charlotte had never seen her before and was completely bowled over by her elegance. I held my breath waiting for her to start dancing. I had wanted it to be a surprise for the others, hence I had not mentioned what Labelle had told me.

The Iron Lady carried her famous father's name, Eiffel. I understood from Labelle that she was now more famous than her father, and people came from around the world to see her. I imagine it was 9pm as she suddenly started dancing. She was adorned with a long cocktail dress sparkling with diamonds and gold. Her eyes flashed illuminating the darkness of the night with rays and beams of light.

"Wow!" we all couldn't help but exclaim to each other, "What a magnificent spectacle." We gasped, the sight was awesome indeed. She was shining from top to bottom and twinkling as she danced. We had never seen anything so awe inspiring. What a dancer she was. What a fabulous sight. We watched spellbound for the next five minutes until she gracefully came to a stop.

Looking down at the masses, we noticed that all the tourists who had come to see her were also mesmerized by her beauty. To imagine that we actually lived just next door to her! What a memory for us to take away when we left Paris. I sighed with contentment as we slowly made our way back to our cozy and comfortable home, happy that I had the opportunity to give my troupe a sight to remember forever.

I knew we had to show Charlotte the apartment and find her a comfortable and safe nook to settle down. I had thought about the situation and had advised them all that it was best not to let Missy meet Charlotte until we were safely installed in London. Although Missy knew of Charlotte's friendship with Fromage, I was not sure how she would react if she realized that we were intending to smuggle Charlotte to London. Missy is a stickler for following regulations.

Fromage and Cara agreed as they too didn't wish to risk Missy vetoing our plans. We were eager to show Charlotte around the apartment. In a way it was opportune that Missy would be in London for a few more days to allow us to get Charlotte used to the premises and for us to discuss leisurely how we proposed to smuggle her over.

"Fromage, oh Fromage," I said to myself. "You do keep me on my toes." On the other hand, it also gave me an opportunity to keep my little gray cells well lubricated. After all, what is life without a few challenges?

Chapter 3
The crossing over

Charlotte soon settled down. She was impressed by our apartment since she had never actually been inside such a warm cozy place, as she kept telling us. Fromage had found her an old shoe box in the back of the cupboard in Missy's box room where she kept her suitcases and old boxes. In the mornings after Missy had left, Charlotte would come out and have her meals with us, enjoying our company. She was delighted that she always had us around. She also came out in the night when Missy was asleep to take a rapid run around the apartment. I sighed with relief. So far so good; Charlotte fitted in seamlessly to our way of living and Fromage was thrilled that he had his good friend finally living with him.

We discovered that Charlotte is actually a Roborovski dwarf hamster. She is very small in size but with a big personality and a sunny, even temperament. Given her tiny stature, we had decided that the best way for her to come to London was by hiding deep in Fromage's shawl. That way Fromage, who was very attached to Charlotte, could keep her safe. The feeling was mutual for Charlotte as well. She had fallen into the habit of lying comfortably tucked into Fromage's large warm shawl whenever she had the opportunity as for example, when Missy and I were watching Dr. House on the box with the lights turned off. Cara had found her a little pink kerchief which she tied around Charlotte's neck, christening her as one of the family. Cara was convinced that Charlotte had to be elegantly clad for her to officially be a member of our family.

As the time to move came closer, Missy made endless 'To Do' lists of all that needed to be accomplished before we took off. A visit to our vet, Doctor Lamoure, was first on the agenda. Dr. Lamoure had been looking after us since I moved in with Missy.

Her clinic was quite close to our apartment and we were in total awe of her. She was a tall and upright woman with gray hair, an attractive profile and eyes resembling those of a sharp Roman Empress. When she spoke she clearly articulated her words. Her grip was very firm and when we were under her eyes we felt we had to sit up to pay attention.

To Missy, Dr. Lamoure was the voice of authority as far as we were concerned, and her wish was our command and had to be followed. They discussed the various vaccinations that would be needed for us to cross over the Channel to London. Despite our reluctance to receive jabs, under Dr. Lamoure's watchful eyes our vocal chords were paralyzed. We were relieved when our session with her was over and were happy to return home with the three passports she gave Missy for us.

Missy said that in the past the UK had insisted that pets, even those traveling from countries within the European Union, had to be in quarantine for six months. Fortunately, the regulations were amended; if not she would never have thought of opening a shop in London as she couldn't dream of keeping us in quarantine that long. I nuzzled Missy. This was another confirmation that she loved us and always had our welfare at heart.

The move itself came about quickly. Monsieur Chevalier had come over one day with three other men in overalls and packed our nice pieces of furniture in a huge container along with other clothes and bits and pieces we would be taking with us. We didn't take much as the apartment was being rented furnished to the young American couple. Apparently, our stuff would arrive in our new cottage the day we arrived. Jacques would be driving Missy's spacious motor-monster, which she called a hatchback, over to London and we would follow in Jacques's mini-bus driven by Genevieve and Missy taking turns; the van contained a good stock of French cheese and wine.

I understood that there were many options to choose from when selecting a ferry from France to England. There are four ferry companies with a combined offering of 13 ferry routes connecting France to England. However, Missy thought it best that we took the fastest route between France and England - that is by driving to Calais and crossing the Channel to Dover, a crossing duration of around one and a half hours.

We were going to leave the following day. Lying awake in my cot besides Fromage in his cot, I said a little prayer that all would go well with the crossing and our secret cargo of one little hamster – Charlotte. I thought I would never get a wink of sleep with worry over Charlotte when I was awakened by Fromage whispering my name.

My concerns surfaced again and I sprang out of my cot instantly, falling over an agitated Fromage. "Are you ok, sis?" he whispered. "Yes, yes. Let's get Charlotte ready before Missy gets up," I whispered back and added, "Best we stay out of the way until we are ready to get into the motor."

Missy had not suspected a thing. I guess she was rather emotional at us all leaving as well and busy making sure the apartment was in mint condition for the new tenants coming later on that day. Jacques and Genevieve had called on her mobile when they arrived and Jacques had brought down our two suitcases. Missy and Genevieve had taken us downstairs to Jacques's mini-van where there was plenty of space for us and we were on our way. Fromage was in his element as he rolled on his back, deeply inhaling the strong odor of the ripe French cheese. Charlotte was hiding safely under Fromage's large shawl holding on to the fur on his neck whenever there was a bump on the road.

We felt a slight apprehension at the border when a beefy French policeman put his long beaky nose into the back of the van to see what we were up to. He had our passports in his hand which he compared by looking at us but he had no clue that Charlotte was safely hidden inside Fromage's large shawl. Missy and Genevieve, who were driving ahead of Jacques, offered the policeman a fresh baguette and a slab of cheese from their breakfast bag. They chatted and laughed with him. This was not the first time the trio had travelled by ferry to London and back.

During the last three months the two vehicles had gone back and forth on the same route as they had been setting up our new place. Sometimes they carried over French furniture and other times they took the produce for the store. So they were no strangers to the French policeman. As far as he was concerned, all the papers were in order so the two cars were waved onto the waiting ferry without too much delay.

The journey itself was relaxing and uneventful, although looking out of our cages from within the ferry, I watched with sadness as the ferry gently pulled away from Calais and headed to Dover.

When we arrived at Dover we did feel a difference. People were speaking with a strange accent. Our vehicle waited in line to exit the ferry, with Missy and Genevieve sitting in front, next to each other. We peeped out of the window, anxious to catch our first glimpse of Dover, our first contact on British soil. It was a very busy ferry port. The change in the environment was palpable as we drove through the town of Dover on the way to London. We arrived in London in roughly two hours, listening to the soft music played by Genevieve on the radio and to Missy's easy chatter and laughter. They were very good friends and much at ease with each other's company.

Missy called from up front, "Wake up, folks, here we are in London." The three of us and Charlotte, who had been lulled by the rhythm of the moving vehicle and soft music to have a good snooze, woke up with a start and peered once again out of the back window. What first struck us were the huge red double-decker monsters chugging along. They looked handsome and solid. "I like that particular shade of red," said Cara.

The buildings in London were very different from the Haussmann apartment buildings which line the boulevards of Paris, uniform in pigments of beige with intricate black iron grills adorning the balconies. The London buildings were handsome but not at all like the environment that we were used to. Somehow everything seemed more solid, lacking the delicacy of French architecture. We soon arrived in Kensington after passing huge parks, a grand palace and museums. We realized that Kensington, where our cottage was located, was a charming neighborhood with fine-looking buildings.

We drove into a large garage and were whisked away to our cottage by Missy, with Genevieve and Jacques close behind us carrying the large suitcases containing Missy's clothes and all our stuff including food and other paraphernalia. The rest of our things were to arrive by Monsieur Chevalier's moving company.

As soon as we arrived in our new home, we started exploring the new premises. Our cottage was very pleasant. It had a thatched roof and white washed walls with abundant greenery in our own private garden. The cottage itself had three levels. The lower level had a small entrance hall, a guest powder room, a cozy living room, a spacious kitchen and an enclosed garden nook where meals could be taken. The upper level, just six steps up, led to two large bedrooms, a small study and a full en-suite bathroom.

Fabulous London, here we come!

Since it was a proper cottage and not an apartment, there was an empty attic just below the thatched roof which was perfect for Charlotte. The attic filled the space between the ceiling of the top floor of the cottage and the slanted thatched roof. The space was awkwardly shaped and difficult for a human to walk around upright, even for slender Missy, but for our small forms it was perfect. Charlotte cheeped with delight when she first saw her new home. We were also pleased since it was an interesting place for us to play detectives and gangsters, our favorite game. There were several high beams in the ceiling of the attic that I could climb on as I am gifted at walking on high narrow beams, unlike Fromage and Cara.

Oh, *Mon Dieu*! I thought. So much space for us to play and relax in unlike our compact two-bedroom apartment in Paris, even though it was chic and elegant. The cottage put us at ease the minute we laid eyes on it. Aunt Florence had maintained her love of France in the touches she had added to the cottage when she lived there.

There was a French inspired garden dining area with French vintage chairs, an arch over an outdoor but enclosed area where the dining table was draped with crisp white linen. There was hemstitch linen napkins and candle-lights with sweet smelling Jasmines were kept in vintage silver bowls.

"Simply divine, refined luxuries," Cara breathed in with satisfaction. What really thrilled us was the back porch attached to the garden dining area overlooking the enclosed private garden. Comfortable chairs and sofas, small low tables and bright rugs scattered on the floor, covered in brown tiles which added a further look of coziness and warmth to the entire environment.

Aunt Florence had made an effort to arrange the cottage in a very welcoming manner. She had agreed with Missy to just leave room for our few pieces of French antique furniture. She had ensured that the beds were fully made with fine Egyptian cotton linen. Aunt Florence is a treasure. She had made sure the cottage was completely livable before she had driven off in a taxi to the airport to take her flight to Paris and then to her home town of Provence.

The cottage had two bedrooms; our room with a very large wrought iron double bed with space for all four of us, if necessary. Aunt Florence knew that Cara occupied Missy's bed and that Fromage and I slept in our little cots in the same room. But sometimes, especially when it was cold or there were flashes of thunder, all four of us slept in the same bed together and this double bed could easily fit us in comfortably. The walls had delicate flowery vintage wallpaper in pastel shades that Aunt Florence had selected.

The second room was a cool blue guest bedroom with plenty of closets and a small adjoining study. The dining room was in shades of yellow and blue with antique French lamps and gilded mirrors. Aunt Florence had imitated Renoir's famous kitchen, with bright yellow and blue tiles with a large working space in the middle. The kitchen was open and spacious, just as the other rooms in the cottage with modern upper cabinets on one side and a window seat where we could look out over the back garden. The cottage had a scattering of bright colored Kilim rugs which made the space cozy and welcoming. To cap it all we had a little porch that we could sit in on sunny summer days.

To give the living room an air of casual elegance, Aunt Florence had decided to furnish it with comfortable wicker pieces with cushions in Chinese lattice. The walls were painted dove white to convey a lightness of spirit with colorful oil paintings in the style of Renoir on the walls in French antique frames.

The garden had plenty of bushes and fragrant flowers. Aunt Florence was an avid gardener and the proof was in the lovely ferns, bushes and flowers beautifully grown in an artistic fashion. There was also a patch where she had grown strawberries, lettuce and rhubarb. This little sanctuary was a delight for Charlotte.

Our furniture, toys, Missy's clothes, music and books had already arrived. Genevieve and Jacques gave Missy a hand in arranging everything before leaving for their own large flat above the new cheese shop. I understood the flat contained a separate large kitchen where they would bake the baguettes and croissants for the shop, and a large basement just like our shop on Avenue de la Bourdonnais in Paris.

The excitement of helping Missy put the last touches to our house was delightful. Cara is the neatest, cleanest and the most finicky cat I have seen in my short life. Her fastidious nature sometimes drives me crazy. We share our litter box and I am aware that she is not too pleased with my toilet manners. She, however, dared not complain out aloud as she considers me her big sister and loves me as much as she adores Missy.

We had not eaten a proper meal for nearly a whole day, so once we were in the cottage, Missy served us a snack which we wolfed down pronto. Missy had this theory that when cats move to a new location, butter should be rubbed on their paws. She believed that when the butter is licked off, the cat settles down comfortably in his or her new environment. So she had rubbed fresh butter on the pads of our paws, both front and back legs. We had no problem licking the butter off! Delicious fresh butter is not normally part of our diet since Missy is careful about us gaining weight.

At the end of a busy day, we were enchanted with the way our new abode looked. The end result was a comfortable and elegant dwelling. My heart swelled as I looked with satisfaction at all we had achieved in such a short time.

But where was Fromage? He had disappeared in the morning when we started arranging the cottage, leaving Charlotte in her new attic to settle down, and he had not appeared when we took a well-deserved pause with a teaspoon each of yoghurt. In the excitement of decorating the cottage no one had noticed his absence. Missy went out searching for him as she did not wish to leave him out on his first night home, and we followed her as she called out, "Fromage, where are you?"

We stopped to admire Solo's lovely garden. To us apartment dwellers, to step out into such a garden was heavenly. The smell of fresh cut grass was blissful. We stared at the large immaculate lawn with a cluster of trees growing wild in one corner. Further around the corner were visible rows of limes and topiary of shrubs. How very artful it all was. We were impressed.

Fromage had not gone far. We found him on the side of the main house garden, deep in conversation with the blue Russian who, on hearing our voices, looked at us with interest.

Missy said, "The famous *Monsieur* Monk, I presume? How are you and I hope our Fromage has not been disturbing you?" Monk got up and with grace, despite his rotund frame, came and rubbed his head on Missy's legs in greeting, twirling around her. Missy was immediately smitten. She patted him on the head and left us, saying, "Dinner will be ready in half an hour, so don't be late."

Fromage scampered up to us, all excited. "Gals, come and meet Monk. I spent the whole day with him. He even shared his lunch with me. He has the most extraordinary stories to tell about Monsieur Solo and his work as a detective. Monk often assists in the investigations, isn't it thrilling! You have to see his house; I have never seen anything so grand. I just took a peak as I wanted to visit when you gals were with me." My dear Fromage, he never forgets we are family.

I took a cool look at this wonder cat while Cara gave him a shy look with her soft blue eyes.

"Enchanted!" said Monk, "Do visit later, since Missy will get worried if you disappear at this moment when she is preparing your dinner. There is a lot to see, and I have to introduce you to my mate Terrance! He is unique, but don't let his soft demeanor fool you! He is one smart chap. Hobbs, his custodian, is a great cook and Terrance is never reluctant to share the delights that spring from Hobbs' kitchen. Hobbs also frequently prepares dinner for Solo when he is at home and dishes out my meals."

"What about around midnight?" he continued. "We could meet here and I will take you inside through my own entrance in the kitchen. Terrance will come up from the basement so that I can introduce you."

Cara looked alarmed! "How can we leave Missy alone in the night?" We have never done so. "It's alright, Cara," I reassured her. "You can put Missy to bed and when she is asleep, we will come over here without disturbing her. I promise we will be back around 2am to sleep until the morning with Missy. You know she never wakes up in the night, so don't look so worried."

With that reassurance, I told Monk to expect us around midnight. What a day it had been! So many changes, so much excitement - what had happened to our usual calm evenings and days in Paris? It suddenly struck me, horror of horrors, "What about Dr. House?" Was I never going to see my hero again? I made up my mind to have a telepathic conversation with Missy about organizing our evenings, as we had done in Paris, watching this show. Surely we could watch Dr. House in London?

We trotted back home, Fromage babbling away. Monk said this, and Monk said that. I was concentrating on what was for dinner when I heard him say, "Inca, Monk says, unlike the calypso and Latina music you adore, he prefers jazz music but he would be willing to watch you doing the salsa."

I gave him my piercing Dr. House stare. "Fromage, why have you been talking about me and my likes and dislikes?"

"No, no," said Fromage, licking my ear, "Monk was just being a friendly curious cat, like we all are by nature. I told him about Cara's love of yoga and your fascination with Dr. House and doing the salsa and merengue."

Honestly, Fromage, this is the limit, I thought, talking about our family to strangers. Before I could say anything further though, Fromage went on about Monk and his passion for chess just like Monsieur Solo. We had never played chess, and I wondered if this was something that I would be apt at given my natural mental prowess. Cara was more interested in taking a look inside Monk's house which she kept calling a manor, though she loyally kept saying in the same breath how lovely our own cottage was. "Cara,

Monk's house is large, but it's certainly not a manor," I explained to her.

"Fromage," I asked, "What is Monk's background? Did he talk about himself at all?" "Yes, he did," said Fromage. "He spoke of Monsieur Solo's love for jazz music and chess. He has been listening to jazz music since he came here at the age of three months, and he is a jazz lover just like Monsieur Solo. He is also mad about chess and knows all the moves. He is very fond of Monsieur Solo and likes to assist him in solving crimes. He also spoke fondly of Hobbs and Terrance. I believe he thinks of them as family, just as we do the three of us and Missy."

"As agreed, let us explore when Missy goes to sleep," I said. "I am sure Monsieur Chess Grandmaster can show us around tonight. Missy will pay her compliments to Monsieur Solo and Hobbs, and introduce us to him formally when she has settled down, I am sure. I understand from Missy's conversations with Aunt Florence on the phone that she and Monsieur Solo had met briefly as children, when he had come home from boarding school and she was visiting Uncle Norman. But they really do not know each other since Missy had her schooling in France and the USA, while Monsieur Solo lived all his life in the United Kingdom. We would have one up on the situation, if we are properly introduced by Monk to the main house before we go there with Missy."

Fromage asked me, "What about Charlotte, Inca? Should we not introduce her to Missy now that we are in London? You promised." he said, as usual placing the entire situation in my dainty but thick strong paws.

I replied, "Have you informed Monk about Charlotte? I don't want to have any difficulties with him. Would he accept Charlotte as we do? I don't want to witness a major disaster."

"Yes, I did and he said that any family member of ours is a friend of his. Charlotte need not fear either Terrance or him," assured Fromage.

"Very well," I said, "Over dinner I will send some waves to Missy about accepting our love for Charlotte and then you and Cara can go and bring her down from the attic. Let's see how Missy will react."

So when Missy set out our cooked fish for dinner, took her share on her plate and sat down to eat, I sat opposite her and looked deep in to her eyes conveying my thoughts on Charlotte as she became absorbed in my gaze. At that point, Fromage and Cara arrived, leading Charlotte to Missy between them, as if introducing their debutant daughter to a ball. Charlotte looked cute with her pink kerchief and I knew in an instant that Missy would take a liking to her.

So I was not surprised when she said, "Where did this little hamster come from? I wonder why Aunt Florence forgot to mention her. What a sweetie! Let me get some food for her."

Looking into Missy's mind, I read that Charlotte had made her mark with Missy and first thing tomorrow Missy would be heading for the pet store to buy Charlotte comfortable quarters to live in. I doubted that she would be banished to the attic; she would probably have her new cage kept in a prominent place downstairs in the cottage. Fromage jumped on Missy's lap and gave her face a loving lick. Missy carefully took Charlotte in her palms and said, "Welcome, little hamster!" She found a shoe box that she lined with newspaper as a bed for Charlotte until she brought her a new cage.

So that is how Charlotte became a member of the Missy family. However, we decided that it was too soon for Charlotte to go out and about with us and that she should stay in the cottage environment for some time until we ourselves became acclimatized to our new environment, particularly the gardens and the home of Monk. My fear was about Monk's reaction to Charlotte, despite what he had said to Fromage. I wanted to talk to him myself and be doubly reassured.

At midnight we carefully padded out of the cottage making sure not to make any noise that would disturb the slumbering Missy. Aunt Florence had put in a new cat flap in the kitchen door leading to the back porch and garden. She had done the same for the front door of the cottage making it easy for us to enter or leave from both the front and the back. However, since the cottage was within a compound enclosed with a high wall all around, it was secure.

Honestly, Aunt Florence had thought of everything, or probably Missy had requested her to have all these facilities attended to before our arrival. I am very aware of Missy's famous 'To Do' lists.

Monk was waiting for us, as promised. One star for Monk, I thought to myself. He is reliable. He led us into the house through his own cat door which led into a massive kitchen three times as big as our own. His house was very large indeed.

I stopped and stared at the high, extravagantly decorated ceiling with its many carvings and designs. The primary feature of the house was its great hall and enormous dining room. The grand hall was handsome, well-sealed with oak. In the salon there were dark leather lounging sofas and a stone chimney, for the moment unlit as it was summer. At the eastern end was a pantry. The large kitchen we had entered through was covered with tiles and it had a furnace and ovens; one large, the other small and two tables. Alongside the kitchen was another small room for baking. The whole house was scattered with Persian carpets that were a variety of colors and elaborate in their design. Cara and I found those carpets exquisite.

"How lovely," Cara murmured whilst walking on the thick pile, and I agreed with her as our paws sank into the carpet.

After walking us around downstairs, Monk led us into a large room he called the library situated at the back of the house. In our eyes, this room too was huge. The walls were lined with books of all sizes and colors in richly bound leather. Monk said that this was his and Solo's favorite room, where they played chess and listened to music, mostly jazz. Apparently Monsieur Solo played chess every Wednesday evening with his friend Inspector Reid, a detective inspector from Scotland Yard. Since Monk was passionate about chess, he never missed a game.

He said casually, "If you gals and Fromage are willing, we could meet here at midnight when Terrance and I meet to discuss cases that Solo and Hobbs are engaged in. I could also teach you to play chess if you like, sometime in the future."

Fromage eagerly agreed. *Hmm,* I thought, Monk is already calling us 'gals', that's from Fromage, I suppose. I was not too interested in chess as I was aware that it was a long, drawn out game. But I was certainly intrigued by the cases he had mentioned. Would this be a chance for me to be a real life Doctor House solving cases? I imagined myself before the white writing board in the corner, solving crimes, just like Doctor House solved his medical problems, with Monk, Fromage and Cara surrounding me, like his medical team.

It suddenly came to me that perhaps Monk was lonely despite his family, and perhaps he was glad to have us as his new cat friends. Actually, though us cats have a reputation for being loners, I can say that this is not entirely true. Fromage, Cara and I love having Missy at home with and us, and when she leaves home, we wait impatiently for her to come back. In the mornings, for instance, while she is getting ready to leave, we all follow her around. Cara and I carefully watch her as she puts on her make-up and selects her clothes for the day. Fromage joins us out of feelings of fraternity even though he has no real interest in make-up or clothes, especially feminine clothes. He only gets interested in clothes when Missy brings home a new beret for him.

I believe the theory of cats being loners developed because we do not like to take orders from anyone, whether we love them or not. But this does not mean that we like to be alone.

A thought suddenly came to me, *'Did Monk fancy himself as a great detective with us as his crime team?'* I wonder if he realized though that I was the leader of his next-door cat pack and wouldn't be too pleased about giving my governance position over to him. Before I could get deeper into these somewhat disconcerting thoughts, I felt Cara gasp as someone padded into the library.

Suddenly a tall, large golden-haired creature entered the room. It was Terrance, the dog belonging to Hobbs. "Calm down, Cara", said Monk gently. "This is Terrance, my friend and partner. You have nothing to worry from him. He likes cats and he will protect you from any harm within these premises or outside if it comes to that. He is our dog guard. Both Solo and Hobbs much appreciate him."

"Will he look after Missy as well?" stammered Cara shyly.

"Of course," said Monk. "We will come around sometime soon so that Missy can meet him."

Terrance eyed us, *'the new neighbors!'*. He gave a nudge to Monk with his black nose. "So these are the pretty lady friends you talked about, ha…Monk?" I couldn't help but notice Monk looking away embarrassed. Very amusing, I thought, so he had mentioned that we were pretty. Well, he got that right. My little sister Cara is very beautiful with her lovely dark nose, ears and mittens contrasting with her dusky beige fur and blue eyes that turned black in the dusk. Cara and I are different in the way we look, but both of us are pretty in our own way.

Terrance went on. "Who is this young lad in a spiffy beret? Is this the young cheese monger you were telling me about, Monk? Very pleased to meet you lovely ladies and young gent," said Terrance, giving us a bow from his tall height.

I studied Terrance carefully. He was a big, powerful dog. I noticed that, although large, he was not clumsy or long in the leg. He displayed a kindly expression and was alert and self-confident. He had a medium length golden coat.

Monk had informed Fromage that Terrance was a golden retriever. He explained that Terrance was affectionate, kind and his best buddy. That Terrance generally accompanies Hobbs wherever he goes and was gentle and even-tempered. That he was smart, observant and good at taking note of situations and accurately reporting all the facts to Monk. That Terrance was also a loyal and courageous friend. That they made a great team as Monk generally didn't move far from home unlike Terrance who brought back lots of information.

Given how at ease Monk was with Terrance, we relaxed too and accepted his greeting in the spirit it was given.

We all made ourselves comfortable on the grand, thick and luxurious Persian carpet in the library. Terrance started to speak about his day. Monk had explained to us that Terrance sits on the floor of Monsieur Solo's office with Hobbs when clients visit to consult. Monsieur Solo's office is in the annex attached to the main house, right next door. But it has no connection to the main house as he wanted to keep it independent from his abode and you have to leave the house to enter the annex. Terrance accompanies them to the office every day. He has the habit of moving around with Hobbs without a leash.

Monk and Terrance, friends forever!

"Guess who came in today to see Solo?" he asked Monk, and without waiting for a response said, "*Señora* Conchita Consoles, the well-known retired opera singer who lives in the vicinity of our premises. She was accompanied by her Pekinese, Polo, who I have met several times in the park. Poor Polo, he was so agitated and was shaking, just like *Señora* Consoles. We had a conversation while Hobbs was getting tea for *Señora* Consoles to calm her down."

"Apparently, *Señora* Consoles had just collected her precious diamond necklace yesterday morning to wear for an event she was to attend this weekend. She had gone out leaving Polo at home, and when she came back, the necklace had disappeared. Polo felt responsible. How could this have happened while he was at home? He told me how ashamed he was that he couldn't protect his mistress's jewelry. He was the only one at home when it disappeared because their houseman, chauffer and butler, Mr. Banks, had left with the *Senora*."

Terrance added, "I reassured Polo that you would solve the crime, Monk." Apparently Monk's reputation as an efficient sleuth among the animal kingdom in the Kensington area where we lived was well established. I wondered if I could take over this position, gently but firmly. I gazed at Terrance and thought, '*Monk does have an advantage over me, having Terrance as his side-kick'*. Would I be able to charm Terrance like I generally do with everyone who comes into contact with me? This may be more difficult, I thought, since all my conquests in the past had been other cats or humans. Well nothing like trying, I thought. Nothing ventured, nothing gained.

"What did Solo say?" asked Monk, rhetorically. "He promised to take the case and asked Hobbs to pass by *Señora's* house with the contract. Solo and Hobbs will examine the house later in the afternoon."

"I would like to examine the house too," said Monk. "Terrance, can you ask Polo if he could let us in to the house?" Fromage jumped, asking, "Can I come too, Monk?"

I was not going to let my little bro outside the compound alone. I didn't think Cara would be up to such an adventure. She was timid and would be nervous to leave the large compound. So I said, "Cara, Missy cannot be left alone, would you be so kind as to watch over her tomorrow night while I accompany Fromage, Monk and Terrance to Polo's house?"

Cara looked at me with grateful eyes. "Yes, yes, indeed, I will," she replied. I stood up and stretched.

"It's been wonderful meeting you both," I said, giving a special smile to Terrance. "But let's go to bed now. It is coming close to 2am. We have a big day tomorrow as I know Missy will want to take us to visit the new premises of the cheese shop."

We said goodnight to our new friends and quickly padded back to Missy, Charlotte and our warm beds. We found that Charlotte's temporary quarters had been placed alongside Fromage's cot and that Charlotte was sleeping as was Missy - both safely in slumber land. We inspected their sleeping heads with satisfaction and in our turn tucked ourselves in bed.

Our new cottage!

Chapter 4
Life gets interesting

Fromage was to visit the new cheese shop with Missy the next morning. Cara and I decided to sniff it out and give them some support. After all, starting a new business is a major venture and Missy knew nothing about cheese, even though Fromage, Jacques and Genevieve would be there as it was their joint venture too. More than anything, Cara and I were curious to see the new shop. The grand opening of the shop was just a week away and they needed all the help they could get.

The mornings are our favorite time of day. We love to be up early and are impatient to get Missy out of her bed. We have this morning ritual, that hardly ever varies, that we all enjoy.

We take turns in waking up Missy. Cara usually starts by gently licking Missy on the face. If this does not work, and sometimes it doesn't because Missy just kisses Cara on her nose and turns away snuggling deeper into the comfortable bed sheets, Fromage comes racing in and jumps on her sleeping figure. This actually gets Missy up, but she cries, "Stop it, Fromage," and goes back to sleep. Then I come in and sit on her chest, pawing her gently on her face, singing my morning purr to her until she finally gets up, and says *'Good morning'* to me and gives my nose a peck. I know that Missy can't resist my morning purr song with its alluring quality.

So we went through our usual morning routine of waking up Missy but this time, when she woke up and said good morning to me, I looked deep into her eyes, conveying our wish to go in to the shop with Fromage and her to help them out. She said, as expected, "Everybody is going to check the new place out. So troupe, let's get moving."

After waking up Missy, she puts the kettle on for tea with lemon and honey for herself and makes sure that we have fresh water to drink and our plates are cleaned and filled with healthy croquettes. We have fun and games soon after. Most often, Cara does her yoga stretches with Missy, while Fromage and I play football with ping pong balls.

Fromage and I are aware that Cara considers herself Missy's special darling. When Missy starts her yoga postures, Cara joins in right away. Cara is athletic, quite agile and able to imitate Missy with her bends and stretches - a treat to behold.

Fromage and I just stick to the 'cat' pose, that is, we tighten our tummies and curve our spines on waking up, true to our cat traditions. To be honest, Fromage did try one or two yoga postures with Missy, but it was more comical than anything else. He resembled an ice cream cone that had half melted in the heat. But Missy, observing his attempts, said "Well done, Fromage," which received a frown from Cara directed at Fromage for trying to invade her yoga session with Missy. To keep the peace, I advised him that it was best to stick to traditional cat Pilate movements that come naturally to us felines and he agreed saying, "I was just trying to show solidarity with Missy and Cara. I really prefer playing football with you rather than doing yoga."

As for me, I love to dance and I take the lead, as I am a good salsa and merengue dancer, while the others try to join in. I am not ashamed to admit that I have attended cat dancing classes with my previous companion, Marie-France. I remember those classes as a joyful experience; there were other cats present with their companions. Such fun!

Olé! Olé! No one can salsa like me!

The first time I performed for Missy, she was amazed. "What?" she said.

I replied, "Why not, Missy? You find this astonishing, you just watch me do the salsa, Missy." From that day onwards, early morning salsa sessions are a given. Just to get attention and listen to the wow factor from the others, I sometimes introduce the merengue. I am the first to admit that I love it when the others admire my dancing skills. After these sessions, we receive one teaspoon of yoghurt each to end our morning ritual.

We follow Missy around until she is ready to leave the house. Though we love following Missy around, we can't tolerate her spraying perfume on herself. The moment he sees a perfume bottle, Fromage dashes out as if his tail was on fire. He claims that perfume would destroy his sense of smell for cheese. I move away as well, simply because I believe the scent of my own hair is fabulous and I don't wish for any other scent competing with it. Only Cara can tolerate Missy's perfume; she relishes the sweet smelling scent. Missy knows that this is something Fromage and I avoid, and more often than not sprays her perfume when she is out of the door. Very sensitive to our likes and dislikes is our Missy.

But since we came to London, with all the excitement, we had not yet got into our morning routine. This morning, with the plan to visit the shop, all we had time for was to hurriedly get our act together to leave the house. Charlotte happily stayed back once I had pointed out to her that someone had to guard the cottage to keep it safe. She didn't really mind. She had plenty to occupy herself with, exploring our comfortable cottage and enclosed garden.

We piled into our cage in the back seat of Missy's car. She had a special cage fixed on the back of her car that was big enough for all three of us. I noticed that all the drivers were sitting on the opposite side to Missy. Very strange! I made a mental note to ask Monk about this. I am sure he knew why Missy's steering wheel was on the left side and everyone else was steering on the right side. As you can see, I am a very observant cat.

While driving, Missy told us that we were lucky that Monsieur Solo had a three car garage. Apparently it was not easy to find a parking space in London. Since he had only two cars, a black Land Rover that he and Hobbs used more for his work and every day running around, and a Jaguar which he used occasionally, he had a place for Missy's car. Aunt Florence had never driven in London, but when she knew Missy was coming over, she had arranged with Monsieur Solo to allow Missy to park in his third spot.

The drive was not very far as the shop was in Kensington. Missy dropped us at the shop and went to park the car in the underground parking.

On arriving at the shop, while Fromage dashed in to inspect the cheese being set out by Jacques and Genevieve, Cara and I took in the shop. We were surprised as it was much more than a cheese shop, unlike the one we owned on Avenue de la Bourdonnais. To start with, it was much larger. The arrangement was light and open. Shelves for cheese and wine lining the walls on one side, and there was an enclosed large glass counter. From what we understood, we would serve two types of baguettes, the traditional French baguette which is the normal plain baguette, and a whole wheat baguette, called 'pain complet' in French, for the health conscious Londoners. Also, plain and cheese croissants all baked by Jacques and Genevieve upstairs were laid out for customers. Yummy…I know how good those are, tempting enough to get us off our protein diet.

Cheese sandwiches prepared with both the traditional and 'pain complet' baguettes would be served from 11am to 2pm either only with cheese or with tomato slices. A fresh green salad would be offered as complementary for the customers who ordered wine and sat down in the cafeteria. Cheese plates and French bread rolls would also be on the menu with French wine, if the customer so desired, or other beverages such as coffee and tea. Different types of Ceylon tea were served; it being understood that the British love their tea.

From the conversation whizzing around, we understood that at first Jacques, a true blooded Frenchman, had refused to accept Missy's idea of serving the baguette sandwiches with French cheese and butter, saying that it was not authentic, never was it served this way in France. But Missy had argued that, while he could have a

74

few 'authentic' cheese sandwiches prepared with baguettes, for the Londoners we had to have some butter since this was England, not France. Genevieve had taken Missy's side and had created a delicious butter based concoction that was to be applied to the hot baguettes before the cheese was placed between the sliced loaves. That even calmed Jacques' patriotic culinary instincts.

On the opposite side, there were tables set up. The whole atmosphere was directly from Provence and very French. Provence interiors are the '*chéri*' of French country interior decoration, relaxed, warm, and stylish.

The shop itself had been designed and refurbished by Missy and Genevieve and looked inviting, very much a part of Provence, where Aunt Florence came from. I understood that Aunt Florence had been a strong influence on the selection of colors and furniture before her departure to Provence. The remodeling and construction was given to a contractor.

The location Missy had selected for the shop seemed ideal. She had selected a neighborhood that was known for food shopping. The area was filled with small shops. The streets were lined with small grocery stores, meat shops and delis. Ours was the first gourmet food store. There were pleasant flower shops and knick-knack shops that generally drew tourists. Right next door was a quaint bookstore and library that also attracted plenty of regular clientele.

The shop had large bay windows and you could see the products clearly from the street. The fresh baguette counter was accessible to people walking by. The hope was that people passing by would smell the fresh baguettes, croissants and rolls, see the different kinds of cheese and wine on display, and walk right in.

Missy, being the business expert, had ensured that there were no other artisan cheese shops in the same area. Good thinking, Missy, competing with another cheese monger would have meant that we would have to compete for the same target customers, and share the local market.

Missy had also negotiated with the French cheese producers and wholesalers to pay them when the cheese was sold. The fact that we already had a successful business back in Paris made it easy to come to this arrangement. Jacques ordered cheese for both shops at the same time.

Our shop in Paris is managed by French staff, and the idea was that Jacques and Genevieve would work in the shop in London with Missy popping in with Fromage from time-to-time until the business established itself. They would then hire additional staff to allow them to go back to Paris and visit London regularly.

Jacques, being the expert on cheese, added that it was important for Missy to hone in on those people who adore dairy, more specifically cheese.

He went on to say, "When you say you are into cheese, it is not just like saying you love cake. From my experience, cheese lovers will read about cheese, talk about cheese, have cheese parties, and take special cheese courses. So true cheese enthusiasts are our ideal customers because they will become regular customers, and even bring their friends."

"I wonder how I will find these cheese enthusiasts," wondered Missy out loud. "I will have to give it some thought," she told Jacques.

Missy was hoping to use her marketing skills to promote the new place as a cool and unique cheese shop and café. Her intention was to use Fromage and his love of cheese as a publicity tool. She would use Fromage as the angle to make the business more interesting and get the attention and publicity required for the new shop.

The shop was to be named after Fromage and he was to be the shop's mascot. This really tickled our Fromage. Finally, not only would he be able to visit the cheese shop weekly or more often than before, but it would also carry his name. The place was to be named 'Fromage and Associates', with 'Associates' denoting Missy, Jacques and Genevieve as well as Cara, myself, and now Charlotte.

"Someday," I told Fromage, "We have to show your new enterprise to Charlotte. She will be so pleased."

Synonymes de La "deuxième" naissance de Fromage Missy était très stricte sur l'hygiène (particulièrement stricte quant aux règles d'hygiène) et elle connaissait par coeur tous les paragraphes et tous les alinéas des documents déposés en plusieurs exemplaires par les services sanitaires. Elle avait d'ailleurs fait une formation en ce sens, apprenant à manier ceci et cela (à préciser) (incollable sur l'étiquetage des produits, le respect des températures ou encore sur la désinfection des locaux). Néanmoins (il n'empêche), malgré toutes ces précautions et la minutie quasi maladive qu'elle mettait à appliquer ces règlements, un petit rongeur prénommé Whitney venait de se faufiler dans la grande salle. Souple comme un élastique, il s'était glissé sous la glissière du soupirail (ou entre les barreaux) tel un champion de limbo et il arpentait la poutre du vieux moulin en suivant un chemin sinueux. Reniflant l'odeur démultipliée du fromage qui emplissait chaque recoin de la pièce de mille et une odeurs merveilleuses et entêtantes, il y associa immédiatement l'odeur du pain (par exemple, le pain au bosphore (pain de campagne à l'huile d'olive, au caramel et aux noisettes)). Il se voyait déjà en train de grignoter la croûte croquante sur laquelle reposerait, tel un tapis de rose, la chair fondante du fromage. Whitney n'en était pas à sa première escapade : en effet, et malgré son jeune âge, ce souriceau avait déjà déjoué à maintes reprises les tapettes à rat et autres pièges déposés un peu partout par des humains machiavéliques et retors, incapables d'affronter en face à face un petit être x fois (à préciser) plus petit qu'eux. A bien y regarder et toute proportion gardée, il préférait un combat à la loyale, à éviter le balai d'une concierge ou d'une ménagère hystérique, tel un fier taureau esquivant les picadors dans cette arène domestique. Whitney venait de se faire la malle du laboratoire de sciences naturelles du lycée qui jouxtait la fromagerie. Il était passé tel un héros devant les hamsters qui dévoraient les km comme Forrest Gump dans leurs roues cylindriques (grosses cylindrées) et avait avisé une fenêtre entrouverte avant de se laisser glisser sur le sol via une gouttière chauffée à blanc par un soleil en très très grande forme, qui dardait de ses rayons puissants la ville grouillante et (à préciser). Il était déjà presque une heure de l'après-midi, l'astre brillant était à son zénith et l'humeur générale était à la paresse. Tout le monde était parti déjeuner, il était (éviter répétitions de "était") donc l'heure idéale pour améliorer l'ordinaire en allant s'octroyer un repas de roi, ce qui le changerait de la maigre pittance servie dans sa cage (que mangent les rongeurs ? Deux, trois carrés de laitue, une pomme toute rabougrie et une demi-tomate qui aura un peu trop séché au soleil).

Exemples de La "deuxième" naissance de Fromage Missy était très stricte sur l'hygiène (particulièrement stricte quant aux règles d'hygiène) et elle connaissait par coeur tous les paragraphes et tous les alinéas des documents déposés en plusieurs exemplaires par les services sanitaires. Elle avait d'ailleurs fait une formation en ce sens, apprenant à manier ceci et cela (à préciser) (incollable sur l'étiquetage des produits, le respect des températures ou encore sur la désinfection des locaux). Néanmoins (il n'empêche), malgré toutes ces précautions et la minutie quasi maladive qu'elle mettait à appliquer ces règlements, un petit rongeur prénommé Whitney venait de se faufiler dans la grande salle. Souple comme un élastique, il s'était glissé sous la glissière du soupirail (ou entre les barreaux) tel un champion de limbo et il arpentait la poutre du vieux moulin en suivant un chemin sinueux. Reniflant l'odeur démultipliée du fromage qui emplissait chaque recoin de la pièce de mille et une odeurs merveilleuses et entêtantes, il y associa immédiatement l'odeur du pain (par exemple, le pain au bosphore (pain de campagne à l'huile d'olive, au caramel et aux noisettes)). Il se voyait déjà en train de grignoter la croûte croquante sur laquelle reposerait, tel un tapis de rose, la chair fondante du fromage. Whitney n'en était pas à sa première escapade : en effet, et malgré son jeune âge, ce souriceau avait déjà déjoué à maintes reprises les tapettes à rat et autres pièges déposés un peu partout par des humains machiavéliques et retors, incapables d'affronter en face à face un petit être x fois (à préciser) plus petit qu'eux. A bien y regarder et toute proportion gardée, il préférait un combat à la loyale, à éviter le balai d'une concierge ou d'une ménagère hystérique, tel un fier taureau esquivant les picadors dans cette arène domestique. Whitney venait de se faire la malle du laboratoire de sciences naturelles du lycée qui jouxtait la fromagerie. Il était passé tel un héros devant les hamsters qui dévoraient les km comme Forrest Gump dans leurs roues cylindriques (grosses cylindrées) et

avait avisé une fenêtre entrouverte avant de se laisser glisser sur le sol via une gouttière chauffée à blanc par un soleil en très très grande forme, qui dardait de ses rayons puissants la ville grouillante et (à préciser). Il était déjà presque une heure de l'après-midi, l'astre brillant était à son zénith et l'humeur générale était à la paresse. Tout le monde était parti déjeuner, il était (éviter répétitions de "était") donc l'heure idéale pour améliorer l'ordinaire en allant s'octroyer un repas de roi, ce qui le changerait de la maigre pittance servie dans sa cage (que mangent les rongeurs ? Deux, trois carrés de laitue, une pomme toute rabougrie et une demi-tomate qui aura un peu trop séché au soleil).
Voir aussi

Traductions de La "deuxième" naissance de Fromage Missy était très stricte sur l'hygiène (particulièrement stricte quant aux règles d'hygiène) et elle connaissait par coeur tous les paragraphes et tous les alinéas des documents déposés en plusieurs exemplaires par les services sanitaires. Elle avait d'ailleurs fait une formation en ce sens, apprenant à manier ceci et cela (à préciser) (incollable sur l'étiquetage des produits, le respect des températures ou encore sur la désinfection des locaux). Néanmoins (il n'empêche), malgré toutes ces précautions et la minutie quasi maladive qu'elle mettait à appliquer ces règlements, un petit rongeur prénommé Whitney venait de se faufiler dans la grande salle. Souple comme un élastique, il s'était glissé sous la glissière du soupirail (ou entre les barreaux) tel un champion de limbo et il arpentait la poutre du vieux moulin en suivant un chemin sinueux. Reniflant l'odeur démultipliée du fromage qui emplissait chaque recoin de la pièce de mille et une odeurs merveilleuses et entêtantes, il y associa immédiatement l'odeur du pain (par exemple, le pain au bosphore (pain de campagne à l'huile d'olive, au caramel et aux noisettes)). Il se voyait déjà en train de grignoter la croûte croquante sur laquelle reposerait, tel un tapis de rose, la chair fondante du fromage. Whitney n'en était pas à sa première escapade : en effet, et malgré son jeune âge, ce souriceau avait déjà déjoué à maintes reprises les tapettes à rat et autres pièges déposés un peu partout par des humains machiavéliques et retors, incapables d'affronter en face à face un petit être x fois (à préciser) plus petit qu'eux. A bien y regarder et toute proportion gardée, il préférait un combat à la loyale, à éviter le balai d'une concierge ou d'une ménagère hystérique, tel un fier taureau esquivant les picadors dans cette arène domestique. Whitney venait de se faire la malle du laboratoire de sciences naturelles du lycée qui jouxtait la fromagerie. Il était passé tel un héros devant les hamsters qui dévoraient les km comme Forrest Gump dans leurs roues cylindriques (grosses cylindrées) et avait avisé une fenêtre entrouverte avant de se laisser glisser sur le sol via une gouttière chauffée à blanc par un soleil en très très grande forme, qui dardait de ses rayons puissants la ville grouillante et (à préciser). Il était déjà presque une heure de l'après-midi, l'astre brillant était à son zénith et l'humeur générale était à la paresse. Tout le monde était parti déjeuner, il était (éviter répétitions de "était") donc l'heure idéale pour améliorer l'ordinaire en allant s'octroyer un repas de roi, ce qui le changerait de la maigre pittance servie dans sa cage (que mangent les rongeurs ? Deux, trois carrés de laitue, une pomme toute rabougrie et une demi-tomate qui aura un peu trop séché au soleil).

The label would be a photo of Fromage in his best blue beret behind a table filled with French cheese; it would be stamped discretely over the entrance, and also on the menu cards.

Missy and Jacques were discussing the expected profit margins, hoping to reach 35 per cent after six months. Until they became familiar with the environment, they would have to lower or raise the prices of the different products. It was Missy's understanding that the overall margins for gourmet food could be extremely high, often nearly 100 per cent. However, since it was their first business of this kind in a new country, Missy cautioned Jacques that they would have to figure it out as they went along.

While Jacques and Genevieve were to directly manage the place, Missy was to concentrate on selling some part of the inventory in bulk to restaurants which wanted gourmet French cheese plates. Missy was explaining to Jacques that she had heard that restaurants could buy £1000 of cheese at a time.

"If we can find restaurants that would buy regularly, it can add some stability to our venture's revenue. If I can only identify 20 restaurants to deliver French cheese to, more people would be exposed to artisan cheese in restaurants, and they would seek them out for home. I will try to introduce French cheese which is not normally carried by any other store in London."

"Turning a passion for French cheese into a successful storefront takes effort and a willingness to adjust an initial dream into a business that works, and we are more than ready, aren't we, Jacques?" said Genevieve. "Our motto will be *'Creating New Tastes and Placing Our Customers First'*," said Missy.

"Meow...," yowled Fromage, jumping on to Missy's lap. What he actually said was, "Hurrah! Very well said."

I was proud of Missy. I knew she was good at her job, but now this was being confirmed before my eyes. Jacques and Genevieve were ideal partners for us. They were authentic food lovers who took their passion for cheese to the next level, as our Fromage. I knew they, like Missy, were not afraid to work hard, and Missy certainly was not afraid to take risks. Like Fromage, they also loved talking about food all day, and this business was definitely for them.

If this venture was a success, Missy would not need to accept other assignments that took her away from us. I was keeping my paws crossed, as that indeed would make our life more bearable since we hated it when she pulled out her suitcase to pack; we knew that meant she would be leaving us. To ensure the shop was a success, she had decided to take a leave of absence of one year from her consultancy firm.

Genevieve asked, "When is the reporter and photographer coming, Missy?"

"Two days before we open," replied Missy. "He is from the prestigious newspaper that has a separate food and restaurant magazine to supplement their Sunder newspaper. We have to have the restaurant spotless and ready. I would also like to have both Fromage and the 'gals' ready for the photos. He talked to me on the phone and said that he would like to have photos of all of us, about 20 in total and let the editor select the ones for the leaflet. He would take some photos at the cottage, some photos of Genevieve

81

preparing the baguettes in your kitchen, and some photos of Jacques and Genevieve in the store."

What? A photographer was coming? I needed Missy to find me a new coiffeur pronto. Surely, after the long journey, I needed to be shampooed and brushed unlike the others who could do with a simple brush with the glove Missy kept for such occasions.

I brushed on Missy's legs, extending my tail up and swinging it back and forth. Genevieve took me in her arms and asked Missy, "Have you made an appointment for Inca?" Good old Genevieve, she got my thought process right in the head.

"Yes," answered Missy. "I hope she likes her new coiffeur. I know she got on very well with Pierre." So that was settled too. I was sure I would never find another Pierre but I was ready to compromise, after all I am a very amenable kitty cat.

Before leaving the place, I made up my mind to see that Missy thought of introducing typical soft French music as a backdrop to when customers entered the shop. Monk was not the only one helping the family business. Fromage, Cara and I would also have a hand in making our own business work.

Monk was waiting for us on the door step when we returned. Was he already missing us?

"Can you come over to my place? Terrance and I have news for you that you may find interesting, given your request to involve you in any developments undertaken by Solo," he said.

"We'll be there at the usual hour," I replied, before Fromage could run off with Monk.

"Remember, we agreed to always have dinner with Missy and behave as normal with her in the evenings, and even go to bed with her as usual and creep away when she fell asleep. I don't want to alarm her," said Cara, who actually wanted to cuddle up to Missy as always until she fell asleep.

"I agree," said I. "Come on, Fromage, let's see what we will have for dinner. I am starving. I can't live on a titbit of cheese."

"Ok, okay," said Monk. "Let's meet at the same time and place as yesterday. I will inform Terrance and I will have dinner with him to calm his impatience. Solo has dinner guests tonight, but I know they will leave early. In the library then around midnight, as before," said Monk, darting off.

After Cara had taken Missy to bed with Cara in Missy's arms like a mother cradling her baby, Fromage and I settled down in our cots waiting for them to fall asleep. When it was midnight, Fromage and I signaled to each other and quietly slipped away crawling softly on our bellies, our padded paws not making a sound, out of the cottage.

We met Monk and Terrance waiting for us in the library.

"Here is the plan," said Terrance. "Polo will be waiting in the garden for us. He too has a little door from the kitchen to go outside. However, I am too big to pass through it. Polo will take the three of you inside the kitchen and show Monk how to twist the French window open from their sitting room to allow me to enter. You have to be very, very quiet to avoid waking up the *Señora*. Polo says she usually takes some sleeping pills, so she would normally be sound asleep. Monk asked about her major dome, Mr. Banks. Polo said that Banks has taken the weekend off, so this is the best time for the visit."

Terrance led the way to the other side of the house, the side we had not visited. The entire main house and large garden, along with our cottage, were enclosed with a thick impenetrable and well maintained hedge nearly eight feet high. However, in one spot not visible to the eye, Terrance had made a hole leading to the other side and to Polo's garden. We all crept through and came face to face with Polo.

Goodness! Was he a dog? He looked a quirky version of a cat with a bug-eyed expression, though I suppose humans would find him appealing and cute. He was small, much tinier than Terrance, with a well-balanced body like mine; actually he was hardly bigger than me. Terrance had told us that Polo was a Pekinese and that he was brave little dog, very affectionate but sensitive about his small stature.

Polo looked at us quickly and said to Terrance, "Thank you for bringing over Monk and his friends. Monk, you will help me, won't you? I cannot understand how someone crept in and stole the jewels when I was in charge. People tend to think that because I am small, I don't take my doggy duties seriously. I have never been so ashamed in my life. You have to help me."

I could see he had a complex about his size, poor Polo. I never could understand why dogs thought about their stature so much, unlike us cats. We are happy to be small and agile.

Monk placed a paw on Polo's sturdy shoulder and said, "Calm down, Polo. Just take a deep breath and help us to solve this case. You know Solo and Hobbs have taken on this case. We are all, Terrance, I and my new friends, here to help you. Let's get in the house quickly and let Terrance in." Polo flashed me a quick smile and said, "Sorry, I don't have time to introduce myself properly. Let's get over this, and you will see the better side of me."

He quickly ran in through the flap door and we followed softly behind him. Monk went to the French window, jumped up and adroitly turned the door handle letting in the fresh air.

"Well done," said Terrance, stepping into the house. I thought to myself, *'Monk is one smart cookie. None of us, Fromage, Cara and I, thought of practicing to open doors and windows.'*

We started examining the house. I followed Monk noticing the inside for the first time. It was a large house, almost the same size as that of Monk's. It was well furnished but everything was covered in dust and not maintained at all. I noticed dust in corners. I wonder if Monk had also noticed it. Cara certainly would have, if she had been with me. Monk asked Terrance to concentrate on the downstairs while he took a look upstairs. I went behind him and we tiptoed around, peeking into the bedroom where the *Señora* was soundly sleeping.

Polo took us to the dressing room where the jewelry was kept and from where the necklace disappeared. Everything was in place, but here again I noticed the dilapidated state of the furniture and the dusty corners. Monk and I went to the windowsill and jumped up on it. No way could anyone have entered this way. There was a steep drop with no apparent footing. There were no large trees either which would have enabled someone as agile as me to jump in by climbing the tree. No cat burglar could or would have entered that way.

I took a quick look and went further down the corridor to a staircase leading down to the kitchen. Monk followed me. Further down there was another door, which Monk nudged open. Here were the quarters of Banks, the major dome. Everything in there was in place but again not very clean. Banks certainly was not an expert cleaner, perhaps his specialty was cooking or he was a good chauffer. His room was empty. Monk was snooping around the dustbin and sorting through the bits of paper in there. The dustbin seemed not to have been emptied for weeks.

He muttered to me, "I wonder if Solo and Hobbs came in here and examined the room." My mind though was more on the rundown house. I was wondering why a rich *Señora* could not maintain her home properly. I wanted to have a chat with Polo to get more details about her without upsetting or letting him aware of my suspicions.

Monk told me, "Inca, let's get hold of Fromage and Terrance and get back home to continue our discussion." Fromage was deep into examining the kitchen. There was a whole full rounded English cheese on an open shelf, with a similar cheese half cut under a glass cover. The way he was eying the cheese, I knew what was going on in his head. He wanted to take a bite of the cheese. I knew he was wondering how the British cheese compared to the French cheese he normally nibbled.

"DON'T even think of it," I told him when I noticed him eying the full rounded uncut cheese. "No way are you going to pinch cheese in Polo's house. You just had your dinner, Fromage."

We left the house through the French window and Polo asked us to wait outside while he banged it shut and joined us through the flap. When Polo joined us, we decided to go over to Monk's library to continue the conversation. Polo trotted along with us looking hopeful and saying to me, "Inca, it's such a pleasure to meet you. I greatly admire your lovely tail."

I thought to myself, *what a gentleman* and replied, "Polo, your tail is very nice too. You must come and meet the rest of my family. I am sure you will like Missy, Charlotte and Cara."

"Thank you," said Polo. "It is unfortunate that my mistress does not go out as before. We used to have such lovely parties with guests always visiting and music and laughter filled the house. We used to visit the exquisite shops and the Kensington Gardens just next door. But now she hardly moves about so I have to count on Banks to take me to Kensington Garden for my walk. But most often Banks has no time for me, so I do not get my daily exercise as before and I miss meeting my friends in the park. It's never fun with Banks as it was with *Señora*. I know she loves me, but Banks just does it out of duty, puffing away at his cigarette, the smell of which I find detestable. For some time now, my *Señora* has been so quiet. She hardly speaks and I have not heard her laugh for ages. She only has me as her companion now and I don't like to leave her alone unless I can't help it. But you must visit as often as you like, and please do bring the rest of your family."

We settled down in the library and I took the same place on the beautiful, luxurious carpet with Fromage by my side while Monk sat on the armchair of Monsieur Solo. Terrance and Polo also settled on the carpet opposite us and we formed a circle around Monk sitting higher up.

Monk asked Polo to relate the day's events, meaning the day of the robbery, not leaving out anything, important or not.

Polo reflected for a moment and started. "It was as any other day except that the *Señora* was supposed to visit her lawyer. The day before, Banks had driven us to her bank to collect her diamond necklace which was in the bank's vault. *Señora* hardly wears it these days as she rarely goes out. But she was to attend an event hosted by a dear friend that she could not say no to and, given the importance of the occasion, she had said that at least she should make an effort for her faithful old friend by wearing some nice jewelry."

Polo continued, "That day, Banks told the *Señora* that, since the lawyer's office was in a very crowded area of the city, was pet-free and he would have to park the car far away until her appointment was over, that I should stay at home, like a good guard dog and take care of *Señora*'s jewelry. Banks was very kind and fixed me a chopped liver dish, my favorite, as a treat for being a good watch dog. Banks is not a very good cook, but he did try to please me as I was having an important job of safeguarding the *Señora*'s jewelry." Polo's face looked even sadder when he uttered those words.

"They came back about three hours later and the *Señora* went up to her room to change, when she found the drawer of her dressing table open – and lo and behold, no diamond necklace. There was pandemonium in the house with *Señora* crying, Banks calling the police, the police arriving and searching the house and coming to the conclusion that a robber had entered the house while we were away and stolen the necklace as the back door was left open. Banks was very sure that he had closed the back door and locked it with a key before he left. The *Señora* very loyally stuck up for me saying that I would never let someone just walk in, but the police looked at my size and whispered to each other that *'this little runt is hardly a dog'*," said Polo, his head sinking almost to the ground.

"Come on, Polo," said Terrance, "None of that now. We have to crack the case, and there is no point wasting energy feeling down in the dumps."

"That's right," said Monk, "Let's crack this case. No room for negative emotions." Polo's head came up, but then he sighed again. "But I was at home and no one came in. I would have noticed if someone had come in and stolen the diamond necklace, even though I could not have defended the house like you could have, Terrance. In any case, if someone had come in, I would have come round to your house, Terrance, and alerted Monk and you that burglars had entered. You know I would have done that," said Polo.

"He has a point there," said Monk. We all looked at each other perplexed.

Terrance, seeing that Polo was returning to his hangdog posture, tried to change the subject. He said "Polo, Fromage and Inca have just moved in next door and Monk and I have not had a chance to brief them about the safety regulations around our compound. Why don't you do that now? It is very important that they know the security code for cats around the neighborhood and you are the best mate at briefings around here."

Polo's head came up and suddenly looked very important. "Yes, our security code is very essential for newly arrived cats, is it not?" he said. "Inca and Fromage, you have to listen very carefully to what I am going to tell you now, and also don't forget to brief the rest as well."

"First let me give you a good idea of our environment. Our row of houses is on Bays Water Road and the front entrances of all the houses down this street face the back of the Kensington Gardens. This is where us dogs are taken for our morning walks. You find many people jogging in the park which is huge and really nice during the day. But the park closes in the night to the public. If you leave through the front door, you will fall onto Bays Water road. Since your cottage is at the back of the house, if you leave by car, you will come out through the underground garage of Monk's house onto Bays Water road. Monk's garage and the *Señora's* garage are next to each other."

"Try to stay within the large garden belonging to Monk or your own enclosed back garden and, of course, you are welcome to visit my large garden but preferably when Banks is not watering the plants. He has a tendency to be mean."

"I can vouch for that," said Monk. "Banks turned the water hose on me the last time." "He would not have dared to do this if I was around," growled Terrance.

"Hobbs had words with him over that," said Monk. Polo looked ashamed again. "I am so sorry, Monk," said Polo. "Quite uncalled for action on the part of Banks and if the *Señora* was in her normal state of mind she would have given Banks a belly full."

"Definitely an unpleasant experience," said Monk. "It is best you visit Polo in the night when Banks is sound asleep. For some reason he does not like cats," said Monk. Monk's large green eyes had a look in them that spelt trouble for Banks. A look that said *'you just watch it Banks, I will get you for that!'* The memory of a cat is not short, somewhat like an elephant's. Cats are able to recognize, often over a very long period of time, not only those who treat them well but also those who mistreat them.

Terrance said, "Yes, but this incident is harmless compared to what you should really be wary of to protect your skin. Polo, you must tell them about Boss." Polo gulped and went on in an urgent voice. "Inca, you cats have to be very careful about Boss."

"Who is Boss?" I asked.

It was explained to us that Boss is the Rottweiler who lives four doors down the street. "He is a large dog, black coated with clearly defined rich tan markings whose powerful appearance does not lack nobility," said Polo. "He considers himself an excellent guard dog and his master seems to be fond of him and he, in turn, seems to be fond of his master who considers him his pack leader. Boss is sturdy and muscular but has a vicious streak. If you have the misfortune to see him, you will recognize him instantly as he is a very arrogant and scornful."

Terrance added, "Inca, you young kitties should stay away from Boss at all costs. He goes for his morning jog every day around 6.30am with his master. They do a one-hour run every morning in the Kensington Gardens and it is best to avoid the front of the street when he is around." Polo said, "For some reason he does not like small creatures, especially cats. In fact, he is rather uppity and does not acknowledge small dogs of my size either."

He went on to describe one awkward situation involving himself and Monk some time ago. Solo and Hobbs were on a case and had to go away to Oxford for a few days. Terrance was leaving with them on this trip. Hobbs had been up since 5am getting the Land Rover packed for their trip. Polo had come to say goodbye to Terrance. At that moment Hobbs had decided to put on Terrance's special collar for his trip and had taken him down to the basement. The front door was left open for Solo who was coming downstairs. Monk and Polo were sitting on the front steps waiting for Hobbs to come out with Terrance in his special collar. Solo generally likes to drive with Hobbs by his side and Terrance always sits in the back.

That morning Boss and his master had set out on their jog a bit earlier than usual. Boss, as mentioned before, has an arrogant personality and he never greets any dog who is not at least his height. He had never acknowledged Polo, though he had seen him often in the vicinity since they both lived on the same street. He has a cursory word with Terrance now and then when they meet. Boss had become friendlier towards Terrance after he discovered that Terrance has quite a reputation as part of the detective team that solves mysteries, and had even been mentioned in the newspaper for some of his brave acts. So Boss now generally says 'good morning' or some such thing to Terrance whenever they meet. But that morning Terrance was not around, only Polo who did not merit a second glance.

Boss first saw Polo and decided that Polo was not worth stopping for a chat and was about to walk off when he saw Monk. Boss had never actually met Monk before and when he saw him for the first time he stopped in his tracks.

"What is a cat doing on my street?" he asked. Monk, who had been cleaning himself besides Polo while waiting for Terrance to come out, suddenly found himself the center of attention. He stopped cleaning himself and slowly sat down trying to absorb the arrogant stranger.

Monk is a big and robustly built cat. But the most striking thing about him is his large green eyes with gold marks. Though he didn't utter a meow, those green-gold eyes seemed to say, "You talking to me, Sir?" Polo's heart started beating like a bongo player mastering his rhythm. He knew from experience of Boss's attitude towards cats. Only some weeks ago he had darted after a cat that lived with the cook further down the street, with murder in his eyes. The orange cat had escaped by the skin of his teeth losing most of his nine lives in the process.

Polo muttered under his breath, "Run inside and disappear quickly, Monk. This guy means business." But it seemed as if Monk had not heard Polo. He continued to eye Boss and his large green eyes seemed to grow larger. Boss was surprised. Cats don't generally stop to attempt discourse with him. Instead, they had the habit of running for their lives.

Out of surprise he took a second look at Monk, noticing his piercing green gold eyes that had absolutely no fear in them.

"What is the meaning of this?" Boss's arrogant manner did not come off so well this time around. He suddenly felt as if the Beelzebub himself was staring at him with beady eyes that looked as if they were on fire. He felt an unknown sentiment clutch his breast for the first time.

"No, it could not be fear. Surely not?" Something whispered in his ear that it was best to leave the blue coated individual who posed as a cat alone. To his amazement, Boss heard himself stutter, "I eh, eh...he, I was just passing by. No, no, I am going jogging actually, you see my Master coming up behind me."

Polo was amazed that he saw surprise and fear on Boss's face and he heard it in his voice. "Don't let me keep you then, toodle doo," said Monk. "Sure, for sure," said Boss and ran off lifting his chest, which had unconsciously receded, almost touching the ground. Polo let a sigh of relief escape his lips. Terrance had come out with Hobbs and Polo had recounted what had just passed between Monk and Boss.

Terrance smiled and said, "That seems to have gone rather well, but, Monk, stay away from Boss in the future."

Monk blinked. "I just established myself as a pack leader, in fact, his pack leader to be precise," said Monk modestly.
"But I wouldn't trust Boss with any other cat," said Polo.

"Yes, I agree," said Monk wisely looking at Inca and Fromage. "You young ones should never ever get close to Boss. If you see him around, the best course of action would be to disappear as fast as you can. Say the same to Cara."

Fromage shouted swaggering, his little beret bobbing, "I am not afraid of anyone, no, not of anyone. I bet Boss will be afraid of me when he sees my glowering eyes too, just like Monk. I will look after my gals, Boss better watch out!" he said, bragging even more. Polo looked amazed at this bravery.

"Can you really fight him, Fromage?" asked naive little Polo. Fromage, lowering his voice to a snarl and curving his upper lip, replied, "I could be a prize-fighter if I really wanted." He added more sheepishly, "And if the 'gals' would let me."

His voice rising again he said, "I can fight anyone, even giants, knock them out with one punch - Boom! Bash! Boom!"

Fromage has a vivid imagination and I sensed that he was picturing himself accosting Boss, in fact several Bosses. Throttling some with his bare hands and others by punching them until he found the entire street littered with hundreds of Bosses lying in various positions out of action, completely dead to the world. *"Honestly, our Fromage is the giddy limit,"* I thought to myself as I noticed Monk and Terrance trying to hide their smiles and Polo looking more alarmed than ever.

"Fromage," I roared, bringing him back to earth with a sudden thump, "We should listen to Monk." I promised Monk that we all would keep away from Boss and I shuddered at the thought of meeting Boss. I knew what bad tempered dogs can do to cats. I had heard of horrendous tales.

To take our minds off the subject Monk asked Terrance to retell one of his adventures with Solo and Hobbs. Terrance reflected a while and said, "Let me tell you folks about what happened a couple of months ago. Monk has heard this episode before, but I am sure he will not mind listening to it again. I know he never gets tired of stories relating to Solo. This is a tale of how Solo helped one of his old university friends out of trouble within a day."

"It happened like this," said Terrance, settling down more comfortably.

"It was a cold winter day and Solo was playing chess with his friend, Inspector Reid. Monk was observing the moves with avid attention while I lazed before the fire. Hobbs was busy in the kitchen preparing our dinner. Out of the blue the front door bell chimed and my friends looked up from the chess board while I cocked my ears, as Solo was not expecting anyone at this time of the night. Hobbs went to the door with me and ushered in a young man similar in age to Solo and Inspector Reid."

"Good heavens, old man," said Solo. "What brings you this way?" The newcomer was a tall, stout young man with a striking and authoritative figure. He was Solo and Reid's mate from Oxford days - Arthur Roberts. Arthur was neatly and well-dressed but had an air of despair in his eyes. Solo and Reid had lost touch with him after they finished university, but their feelings of camaraderie had not diminished over the years.

For a moment Arthur couldn't speak out loud and Solo spoke to him and said, "Take your time, old man. You have come to right place, if you want your problems shared and solved."

Slowly Arthur started to speak, "Since I left university, unlike some of my fellow mates who have private income to fall back on or a profession career, it became evident to me that I needed to work besides my life's ambition to become a writer. I soon realized that a new writer needed a breakthrough to make it a lucrative profession and I was far from that stage. So, when I saw an advertisement for a private tutor for a foreign business tycoon's son visiting England from Latin America, I jumped at the chance since the remuneration mentioned in the advertisement was good and included lodging. I applied for the position, was interviewed and given the job. I was pleased because I could earn a comfortable living while also concentrating on writing my book in a quiet and luxurious environment."

"My ward was the young son of the foreign business tycoon who will remain unnamed for the moment and who I shall call Mr. X. He had a large mansion in Sussex and I took the train down soon after and was given spacious lodging and meals of good quality and high standards," he continued. "I soon settled down to work. My ward was 17 years old, a young and intelligent, but lazy, young lad and in my opinion, rather too used to the good things life has to offer. Nevertheless, despite his lazy attitude towards learning, he was a friendly and good-natured chap. I tried my best, and the father seemed to be satisfied with the progress I was making. In this calm atmosphere, my writing was also going well and I was pleased with my lot."

"A few days ago the father went on a business trip leaving the young man in my custody and the house in my care. Last night, I woke up in the night and came downstairs to find the front door unlocked and the house empty. I searched the house, not feeling particularly perturbed but the lad had disappeared. Although unusual as he had never done so before, I thought that he may have gone out without wishing to disturb me. Leaving the door unlatched seemed to be rather irresponsible, but I thought nothing of it and, though slightly concerned, went back to bed."

"The next morning when he hadn't still returned, I realized that the situation was more serious than I had originally thought and started to get worried. It has been one day now and he has still not appeared. I am at my wit's end. 'Should I call the police?' I thought to myself, but I am not sure Mr. X would appreciate me bringing in the police without consulting him. I am aware that he does not like publicity. I have tried to call him but his mobile phone is switched off. He did warn me that he may not be reachable for a few days. I suddenly thought of you and after looking up your address, I immediately took the train and here I am. Can you help me?" he said, looking very worried indeed.

"Let's get more facts," said Solo. "Is the house deserted or are there other people in the house other than the young man and yourself?"

"It was the young man, the Italian cook, a Philippine houseboy and me. The cook and houseboy come in daily but only the son and I live in the house when the father is away," he replied.

"What was his relationship like with the help, and did he have friends visiting?" asked Solo.

"I have been with them now for two months but they kept very much to themselves. From what I understood, the father brought the son over to England to prepare him for entrance to university so I don't think that he had much time to socialize and make friends. We had a very routine lifestyle of coaching, jogging around the nearby lake and reading English books for entertainment. The father was keen to see his son improve his English and concentrate on his entrance exams to be held at the end of the year. The young man was civil to the cook and the houseboy, but I never noticed that they were friends. However, I do recall that he would go swimming with the houseboy at the local swimming pool whenever he could. That did not happen very often though," said Arthur in reply.

Solo said, "Hobbs, serve a plate for Arthur as well and get the guest room ready as he will stay with us tonight. Tomorrow we will drive him to Sussex to take a look at the house. If the young man is back at home by the time we reach it, so much the better. Let's leave early to avoid the traffic."

"Hobbs drove us to Sussex the next day. When we arrived at the mansion, there was no one around other than the houseboy who had just come in. Arthur informed Solo that the cook came around noon and lunch was generally served anytime between 1pm and 2pm They generally managed breakfast by themselves."

"It was 9am when we arrived and Solo asked Arthur to take us to the son's room for me to sniff some of his clothes to get a good scent of him. I smelt the pajamas, looked up at Solo and took another sniff at it with my body quivering. Solo knew I was ready.

He said, "Go find him, Terrance." I knew immediately that he wanted me to trace the owner of the pajamas that were lying on the floor. I went sniffing at a speed, scenting and circling. His scent was practically all over the house; what was interesting was that I found the scent on the sneakers that the houseboy was wearing and circled him several times looking at Solo. Solo reads me like a book. Solo has worked with me before, and we understood each other with no difficulty."

"Solo clapped a hand on the houseboy's shoulder and said, "We need to have a chat, young fellow." The houseboy, who was called Ramon, looked very nervous. But Solo has a way about him, so we found out very soon that, for the price of a pair of expensive sneakers belonging to the young man, Ramon had agreed to take him on his scooter to meet some friends he had met at the pool. Ramon had actually driven the young man there on the scooter and knew where he was."

"Without further ado, we got into the car with Ramon and headed back to London. The location to which Ramon guided us was a dirty old alley situated behind the piers which line the north side of the river to the east of London Bridge. Between a shop that sold spirits and an abandoned Chinese laundry down a steep set of stairs was a much used door with the paint flaking off. The place reeked of spirits and smoke and, seeing the place, Solo asked Ramon to watch the car while we went inside."

"We saw bodies lying in different positions smoking from long tubes. Arthur shuddered visibly. An old man with gnarled hands and a decrypt bearing descended upon us. He was in charge of the place. Solo quickly passed some money to the gnarled hands which snapped it up. Solo asked, "Have you seen a young boy of Latin origin who came in last night? Is he still here?" Without hesitation the old man pointed at the room in the corner and whispered in a hoarse voice, "He is still in there with some toughies who brought him. I don't think he realized what he was getting into because I heard him asking to leave, but he was roughly shoved aside."

"Arthur gasped, shocked at this news. Solo pushed the door open and charged in with us close behind him. We found the young man haggard and unkempt but he wept with joy at the sight of Arthur and his friends. Solo roughly said, "Arthur, take him and go back to the car." The toughies reacted but one look at my snarling jaws and my broad shouldered companions shut them up. I can be very threatening when I have to be. We had the young man back in the house within an hour but without his expensive Rolex watch which had mysteriously disappeared during the night."

"This was no great case for Solo, but Arthur was extremely grateful. It saved his job and restored his sanity. The young man had learnt a good lesson and with great emotions thanked Arthur for coming to his rescue. Both the son and Arthur wisely decided to keep the father in the dark and reported that his watch went missing at the swimming pool. A missing expensive watch was better than a missing son. The young man was glad to have gotten away with just that."

I realized that Terrance was an invaluable helpmate to Solo. No wonder Monk respected Terrance. He must be very useful to Solo and Hobbs in their line of work.

"Terrance, did this type of detective work come naturally to you?" I inquired, very much interested to know how he developed his detective skills. I had known several doggies that lived in our apartment building in Paris, but I had never come across one as smart as Terrance before. My doggy mates, many of them my former neighbors, were snazzy dressers and often visited Pierre to be regularly coiffed. This was natural as they were Parisian doggies living in the 7th district and they took great pride in walking about well dressed, even accompanying their human friends to restaurants. However, my general impression of doggies as characters who wagged their tails a lot and barked incessantly at everything and nothing was gradually changing after my brief encounter with Terrance. Now I understood why Monk had him as his best friend, 'mate' as he called him.

"To be honest, from a very young age, I was sent to a Canine Search and Rescue Academy by Solo," said Terrance. "As soon as I was brought home by Hobbs, Solo believed I was gifted and decided to send me to an exclusive rescue academy. I was the youngest trainee and I considered the training zone as a glorious playing field. It had sliding boards, ladders and platforms, tunnels and pass-throughs lined with benches, tire swings and ramps. Learning was fun for me and soon I started winning medals as predicted by Solo. Both Hobbs and Solo were often with me during the training, and I never gave them a chance to regret the time and money they spent on me."

He laughed and said, "I am the first to admit that I was not always so calm and respectful. In my younger puppy days, I was quite a handful, eating Hobbs' shoes and chewing everything in sight. When my training was complete, I was altogether a different character. But it was fun all the same, being a brat. I still let go sometimes. You should hear me sing when riding in the car with Hobbs."

Monk smiled. "Sounds more like howls to me, old man," he chuckled. Terrance wagged his tail and joined in the laughter. *'What pals they were'*, I thought. *'Good and loyal friends with no complexes'*. These were the kind of friends Missy and our family need. Aunt Florence was right about Monk. He would be a good influence on Fromage, too. Someone that Fromage could look up to and have boy-to-man talks with from time to time.

"Let's break up now," said Monk. "Terrance has loads of similar stories that he can tell us later. We all need our sleep and time to ponder on this perplexing puzzle concerning the *Señora*'s missing diamond necklace. I feel more at ease that Solo and Hobbs are also investigating the case. So let's meet tomorrow."

What a fun evening this had been. I was truly interested in hearing more Solo-Terrance-Hobbs stories. We all got up slowly, deep in thought, and Fromage, Polo and I left, Polo crawling through the hedge back to *Señora*, and Fromage and I back to Missy and Cara.

Cara opened her eyes when we came in and whispered, "I was getting so worried. What took you so long?"

"Go back to sleep, Cara. I will explain all tomorrow," I said and stretched out at the bottom of Missy's bed while Fromage curled into his cot next to his sleeping friend Charlotte.

The next morning, after our usual morning wake up performance, we went to the kitchen to watch Missy cook our breakfast. Over breakfast, Missy told us that the television man was coming in to install the satellite dish so that we can watch Dr. House in French as we did in Paris.

"Goody," I said with relief. It had not been necessary for me to concentrate telepathically with Missy; she had thought of this on her own. She also said that, after the television man had left, she would be going into the shop alone to work with Jacques and Genevieve in organizing the store and we should stay at home. She would come back in the afternoon to take me to the hairdresser.

I thought this was a good idea as the night vigil had made me sleepy and I wanted to catch up on my beauty sleep as well as have a "pow-wow" with Fromage and Inca about what happened that night. Fromage wanted to keep Charlotte informed of all that happened. Charlotte asked, "When am I going to meet your new friends?"

"Very soon," I replied. "Be patient."

When Missy left to work, I explained to Cara and Charlotte about our nightly sojourn to Polo's house, about meeting Polo and investigating his house and all that had happened, with Fromage chipping in here and there. Cara listened with her blue eyes shining.

"What do you think really happened?" asked Fromage.

"I noticed something," I said and, looking at Cara, explained about the dilapidated and dusty condition of the furniture in such a magnificent house in Kensington. "What do you make of it?" I asked, as this had been on my mind during the night.

Cara said, "Perhaps the famous opera singer is broke and doesn't have enough money to refurbish her house."

"It most certainly is a possibility," said Fromage.

"Do you think it is possible that she stole the diamond necklace herself?" I said. "Or pretended that it was lost but took it with her when she left with the drawer open to convince the police that a burglar had robbed her?"

Fromage said that we should talk to Terrance and Monk about this theory. "Alright, we can, but let me introduce the proposition myself," I said. "Okay Fromage?"

"As you say, sis," said Fromage, "You are in charge." I kissed him on his nose and went up to bed to catch up on my sleep while they chased each other around the cottage.

Then Missy got back, leaving Cara and Fromage behind, I climbed into the cat cage attached to Missy's bicycle and away we went for my hair cut.

What a location! It was way larger than Pierre's parlor in Paris. The place was 3,000 square feet spa in Chelsea. There were several other dogs and cats, some of them rather snooty with their noses in the air, waiting their turn in the posh location when we entered. The place boasted that it offered the world's most exclusive selection of pet grooming services and indulgent spa treatments to ensure that your pooch or pussy pal looks and feels the very best. Honestly, I thought that was too much. I preferred Pierre's unfussy but neat little parlor.

Nevertheless, I had to admit that I was pleased that Missy had selected the full package for me which included full body grooming to fresh breath treatment. She left me with a young lady, promising to pick me up in two hours. Two hours of pampering... sheer bliss. Wait until I tell this to Cara, she would be so jealous.

The treatment was similar to Pierre's, that is, the shampooing, drying, and then hair and nail trimming. In addition, I had a fresh breath treatment that I was not totally convinced I needed and, for the future, not necessary. I thought of the need to convey this to Missy. But even as the thought flashed through my mind, I knew this would not work as Missy has fixed ideas about my teeth. Apparently she had read in a cat care magazine that Siberians should have their teeth checked regularly as they have a tendency to gum and teeth disorders. *'Drat to that cat magazine,'* I thought.

There were five 'gals' working in the spa so I would not perhaps see the same hairdresser next time around. She had been very pleasant, admiring my coloring and the texture of my coat, murmuring softly to me throughout my treatment. Missy picked me up and said admiringly, "You do look elegant, Inca. I know you miss Pierre, but that's because you knew him for so long. You will soon get accustomed to this place. Your new hairdresser, Amanda, is very nice isn't she?" I couldn't disagree with her, feeling a pang of guilt about my disloyalty to Pierre.

Spa treatment! For sure I am worth it!

Chapter 5

Something smells fishy

To my great delight, we were able to watch Dr. House when we returned home from the spa. Cara and Fromage had their coats brushed by Missy and their nails cut. So we all looked very well groomed that evening watching Dr. House and enjoying a bit of yogurt with Missy, who was having a light supper of soup herself. Only Missy and I are addicted to Dr. House. Fromage was lying on his back with his paws in the air, close to us, dreaming of his cheese shop and giving a long winded description of his new cheese venture to Charlotte. Cara cuddled next to Missy, sound asleep. Missy and I were glued to the television screen enjoying how Dr. House unraveled the mysterious ailment of his patient. I imagined myself for a moment in Dr. House's brilliant shoes.

After House went away from the box, Missy decided that we should have an early night since the photographer and journalist were visiting us the next day. So, after she had taken a bath while we played with the water in her bath tub and she had gone around closing the windows, we went to bed with Missy. She was tired from running around getting the shop ready with Jacques and Genevieve. Fromage, Cara and I, knowing that our sleep would be broken, were determined to have a good nap before the clock struck midnight. During bath time, Charlotte had gone to her new cage to practice her spinning laps. I have never known anyone so keen on exercising. I whispered to her that she should rest too as we had decided to take her with us to introduce her to the rest of the new clique.

We slipped out at midnight and entered Monk's silent house. Charlotte was on Fromage's neck clinging on to the fur on the back of his neck inside his shawl. Monk and Terrance were waiting for us in the library. Fromage introduced Charlotte as his best friend to both Monk and Terrance, after which we made ourselves comfortable. Monk was cool about it and a perfect gentleman in his welcome of Charlotte to his abode.

Monk told us that Terrance had reported that Solo and Hobbs were on the case. Solo was talking with his detective friend to see what the police had done so far. Hobbs was going from house to house in the neighborhood to see if anyone noticed anything unusual around Polo's house that morning. So far the search had not resulted in anything concrete as the neighborhood was very quiet and not many people noticed what was happening next door, given the sizes of the compounds. If someone came in from the back entrance nothing much would be noticed. But everyone Hobbs had spoken to had assured him that no unknown faces had been seen lurking in the vicinity.

I gently asked Monk and Terrance what they knew about the *Señora*. I mentioned to them that Polo had said that she did not move around as before and was mainly cloistered in her house.

"Why was that," I asked?

Monk explained the situation, "Polo has gone through ups and down like the *Señora*. Despite his pedigree, because Polo's first owner was an elderly lady who lived alone, when she unexpectedly passed away he was housed by the local authorities in a rescue home."

I shuddered. *How terrible*, imagine this happening to one of my family. Poor, poor old Polo. He remained in the shelter for some time, when the *Señora*'s husband came to the rescue home by chance, not exactly to pick a dog, but because he was accompanying a friend who had come to look over the home.

Terrance continued, "When he saw Polo, he was immediately smitten and brought him home as a companion for the *Señora*. She was at her peak as an opera singer at that time, constantly travelling around Europe and the rest of the world to give memorable concerts. Both the *Señora* and her husband, Raoul, loved Polo. Polo accompanied the wealthy, well known couple and had the opportunity to travel around the world. He was pampered and spoilt by both the *Señora* and her husband who was a decent fellow."

Raoul had three passions in life. He loved the *Señora*, he loved playing polo and above all, he loved mountaineering. He named the little rescue dog Polo after his favorite game. He had tried many times to entice the *Señora* to accompany him and his friends on these mountaineering trips. But she loved her comforts and never agreed to go with him. His dream was to climb Mount Everest and he was excited about the forthcoming climb that was being organized by his club. He bid farewell to Polo and his dear *Señora* promising to return soon.

But unfortunately things didn't go as planned. Sadly, the *Señora's* husband had an accident on Mount Everest and passed to the other world. Since that time, it has been only Polo and the *Señora*. Banks was hired when the *Señora* withdrew more and more into her shell. Her heart had been broken on hearing that her beloved Raoul had been lost on Mount Everest. She didn't even have the energy to walk Polo to the park and left the house only when she was forced to. Her world had been wrapped around her husband who took care of her every need and when he suddenly disappeared, she felt completely lost. All her glory seemed to have no meaning.

Conchita Teresita Estevan Consoles, more commonly known as *Señora*, is a sensitive lady of artistic temperament with a beautiful melodious voice. She has a delicate personality, a keen sense of humor and is kind and generous, despite her wealth and standing in society. Of late, she has fallen into the habit of slinking through the corridors of her mansion; her tall slender silhouette floating slowly up and down the corridors. She walks, or rather she wanders, around without any real purpose, taking the same path endlessly, as if guided from within by some dark force.

She, the famous opera singer acknowledged by Her Majesty for her concert performances, is now a shadow of her former self. She was, not so long ago, notwithstanding her gentle nature, a confident woman, self-assured in her talents, proud of her amazing gift to sing like a nightingale making her audiences listen to her mesmerized.

But she has now become unrecognizable. Who would have believed meeting her today that she is the same grand dame who had so many press clippings in her name praising her talent and achievements as the most famous opera singer in Europe? The shell left behind is of a woman half the stature of the *Señora* the world knew and Polo loved.

The once so warm and friendly *Señora* had disappeared. She moves around not in her sophisticated outfits but covered in several layers: a large gray muffler covering her face up to her nose, and a large overcoat belonging to her husband that covers a thick, heavy and baggy dress, sunglasses and hat with her face nearly completely covered. The padded outfit allows her to isolate herself from the world. Now, her empathy had given way to almost complete apathy.

Naturally, Polo is very worried about the *Señora* and is hoping she will come out of her shell and start living life again. Polo is constantly asking us to invite Solo to introduce his friends to her, but Solo is so busy with his sleuthing and chess tournaments that the occasion has not yet risen.

I looked at Monk wondering how I could bring up my observations delicately when Fromage burst out, "Inca suspects *Señora* of having taken the necklace."

"Fromage!" I said, giving him a stare.

"Oops!" said Fromage, and started licking his tail vigorously, avoiding my eyes.

Monk looked at me, "You are an observant little pussy cat, Inca. I saw you looking at the house and furniture carefully yesterday. Yes, the furniture is in a bad state and the house is barely clean and Solo had exactly the same thought when he visited the *Señora*. Hobbs and Solo were wondering if *Señora* was hoping to collect the insurance money as she was in a bad financial state. His detective friend had been working on these lines as well. Since *Señora* is now Solo's client, he has to find out the truth and, if this is the case, avoid a scandal. He owes it to Raoul who was his friend. Imagine what the newspapers would say, if the *Señora* is suspected of stealing her own necklace to claim the insurance money!"

"This is a suspicion only and Solo is making discrete inquiries within the financial circles to find out if the *Señora* is really having financial difficulties. It is well known that Raoul was a very wealthy man and the *Señora* herself, because of her reputation as a renowned opera singer, has amassed her own fortune over the years. She is now retired but is still very famous in her own right. The diamond necklace that was stolen was valued at nearly one million pounds."

"What? One million pounds?" I said. I thought to myself, *'Missy and I could take our little troupe and retire in the south of France with that kind of money'*.

"Be careful though, you three. We have intentionally not mentioned this line of thought to Polo, who would be devastated. He loves the *Señora* so much that, if he even thought we were thinking along those lines, he would be so upset with us that he would not speak to us ever again." We gave Monk our solemn oath not to mention any of this conversation to Polo with Fromage promising twice over, given his habit of blabbing.

"What will happen to Polo, if this is really the case?" Cara asked. We all looked at each other. We couldn't let him go back to the rescue home. It would be just too much for him to cope with. I was thinking thoughts I had never had before. I said to myself, *'How fragile our lives are'*. Imagine other animals in rescue homes and how they must feel without a loving human companion in their lives. I could see tears starting to well up in Cara's blue eyes and quickly tried to change the subject by telling Monk and Terrance that Fromage had been selected by Missy to be the mascot of our new shop.

This immediately made Fromage preen and start talking about his new café and shop, explaining about the cheese, wine and other goodies that would be on sale in his shop. "You know my Papa, who also was born in a French Cheese shop, always said that, since this kind of a business has a physical location, the bulk of the marketing is done by having a beautiful storefront. People walking by notice the storefront and become curious. Those who live in the neighborhood and pass by can also become regular customers. Over time, such a store can build a steady following in the neighborhood. Our Missy said that there was a huge office block and an exclusive clubhouse whose clients would surely be interested in the fine wine and French cheese in our shop."

Cara excitedly started talking about the Provence style decoration of the shop. She boasted that the Provence region of France has beautiful Mediterranean country style crockery in yellow ochre and green and that Missy had stuck to this traditional color scheme. The walls were adorned with some beautiful traditional pottery pieces in the same colors. She ended by asking Terrance and Polo to visit the place to see for themselves.

In this manner, the time passed quickly with all the questions posed by Monk and Terrance about the new shop. I finally said, "It's 2am. It is time to go back to bed. It's best to sleep on the case; let's hope Solo and Hobbs come up with something new."

That night, Fromage had agreed with Monk to learn how to play chess. We all decided to go and learn about this game that seemed to captivate the hearts and minds of Monk and Solo. What made them sit quietly for hours looking at the black and white pieces on this little checkered board? There must be something not visible to the eye.

Charlotte made a surprising statement. "I know how the game is played," she said. "I have watched it played by the students in the science lab where I lived. Although I never got a chance to play myself, I have watched it several times and it can be quite an interesting game, I would give anything to play it."

Monk set up the chess board with little figurines, explaining to us who they were; the king, the queen, the knights, the rooks and pawns, and their roles in protecting the queen. He then explained the rules of the game.

We decided to go through the moves a few times to get the hang of the game and sat beside Terrance and Monk watching them as they played against each other. We made our recommendations on which figurine should be moved to get the other's queen. Yes, indeed the game had a manner of taking our attention.

Fromage asked Monk, "Would you play against Charlotte? She has been whispering to me that she is eager to play a game after having watched it so long from the sidelines in her old home in Paris."

"Yes, certainly," said Monk. "But since it is her first time, let her play against Terrance who generally loses to me." So he set up the board again and they each took their place to play against each other. Charlotte versus Terrance!

Terrance invited Charlotte to make the first move, which she did cautiously. Terrance made a counter move and Charlotte bent over the board deep in thought and then made her move. This was repeated a few times by each of them and then a few more moves later, Terrance gave an unexpected exasperated sound.

Monk whispered to us, "Terrance is in trouble."

What? Is it possible? Charlotte had the upper hand? Check mate! It was over. Terrance, with a deep look of respect at Charlotte, knocked over his king.

"Where did you learn to play like that, Charlotte?" he asked. "Well done, let's play again, please." We were all impressed. *Could it be beginner's luck? Was Terrance purposely giving the game away to be kind?*

It was not the case, they played again and Charlotte once again beat him. Terrance was a good loser, I must say. He had nothing but praise for Charlotte and said, "You are a champion, Charlotte." Fromage preened as if he was the one who had won the games. What an exciting evening. Monk said he was looking forward to playing against Charlotte.

We padded back slowly to the cottage. We thought of Polo and I suddenly had an idea. I turned to Cara and Fromage and said, "Why not get Missy to meet the *Señora* and Polo?"

"You mean like getting Missy to adopt Polo like she did Charlotte and me?" enquired Fromage, blinking his eyes.

"Possibly," I said. "At least Missy would make sure Polo was not abandoned again. I could work on her mind, couldn't I? In any case, knowing Missy, she would probably not need any prompting from me. If not with us, she could at least ensure he found a loving home."

The next morning Missy woke up even before us and was attacking the little cottage with a vengeance. We sleepily trotted behind her, as she moved our dreaded adversary, the noisy aspirator, around the floors having removed the kilims which had already been dusted and were airing on the patio. Very soon the parquet floors were shining and our house was spotless with fresh flowers and foliage arranged artistically by Missy in cut glass vases placed strategically all over the cottage. Cara and I admired her handy work. Missy was a genius in the household arrangements department. Charlotte's new quarters were also shining as Missy had said that she could participate from her cage.

She then started on us, giving both Fromage and Cara another good brushing, wiping their eyes with damp cotton. Fromage couldn't stop jumping with excitement. Missy had pulled out a brand new blue beret which she placed at an angle on Fromage's little head. He kept licking Missy on the face while she was adjusting his beret and she laughingly said, "Stop it, Fromage. One thank you lick would be enough."

Fromage looked at Cara and me and said, "Well, how do I look, gals?" He did look spiffy! Missy had also bought his friend Charlotte a small pink beret just like Fromage's. How kind of Missy not to leave out Charlotte. Charlotte couldn't stop her little nose from quivering with excitement. Since I already had been to the hairdresser the day before, Missy just cleaned my eyes, adjusted my silk neckerchief and said, "There you go, young lady, all ready for the photographer."

We heard a knock on the door and I went running ahead of Missy to welcome our guests, as I generally have the habit of doing. I love welcoming guests to our abode. Unlike Cara and Fromage, the idea of saying *'howdy'* to guests gives me the greatest pleasure. Missy opened the door. On the doorstep were a young man with shaggy hair and a camera hanging on his shoulder, and a young lady in jeans. Was this the journalist? Missy welcomed them in and offered them tea. The table had been set with French cheese from our shop and fresh croissants and baguettes freshly baked by Genevieve and just dropped off by Jacques. They couldn't help being pleased. Who could resist our cheese and patisseries prepared by Jacques and Genevieve? No one that I know of!

"Please help yourselves," said Missy. After a sumptuous breakfast, with both the journalist and photographer complimenting Missy on the quality of the food, the photographer started to take photos of Missy who was sitting on the sofa. When the journalist found out that Fromage was to be the mascot, the photographer took several photos of Fromage in different poses, some with him sitting before a table laden with different types of French cheese that would go on sale, arranged tastefully around him.

didn't go unnoticed. We never do for very long. There were several photos taken of the three of us posing together and of us sitting around Missy. One was taken with me sitting on Missy's shoulder at the back of the sofa, Cara on her lap and Fromage sitting by her side in his beret and shawl.

Cara whispered, "Doesn't my Missy look nice."

I whispered back, "She is also our Missy, Cara," but the statement didn't wholly register as it generally doesn't when it comes to Missy.

Cara tends to take over ownership of Missy, and Missy's constant treatment of Cara as if she is still a baby doesn't help this equation. Missy was in her usual attire of navy blue pants, a white shirt tucked in, a thin leather belt around her waist and a string of small white pearls that had been Aunt Florence's gift to her around her slender neck. She wore a matching pair of pearl ear studs that she had bought herself. On her feet were well polished, comfortable knee length Italian boots with low heels. In my eyes, Missy looks lovely all the time.

Family photo for the newspaper

After the busy morning in the cottage, Missy went off with the photographer and reporter to show them the shop and take further photos of Jacques and Genevieve working in the kitchen and in the café.

We slipped back to the lazy rhythm of summer days in our comfortable cottage. It's as if Charlotte had been part of our lives forever. She told us that she felt as if at last she truly belonged part of a family. She had the full run of the cottage and when she wanted food she just entered the cage and helped herself. Missy ensured that she had the best food at hand all the time, and no more dry crusts from the guardian at her former High School. When she wished to exercise, she either did laps around the circular part of her rotating cage or dashed about the cottage. She spent a lot of time exploring the attic as well.

A few days later, we went over to see what Monk was up to. He was at his usual place near the hedge as if he had been waiting for us. He said, "Hobbs had left some delicious salmon which you could share." We padded after Monk thinking how generous he was. We entered the kitchen through the large flap door and tasted the delicious fish.

"Tasty," said Cara, "but not as nice as Missy's fish. You should come over one day and taste her cooking." I am not picky; I wolfed down a piece of salmon.

Cara, even at home, plays up to Missy when the food is served. She needs to have Missy watching over her when she eats, though we have noticed that she manages perfectly well when Missy is not around. Even our evening spoon of yoghurt has to be fed by Missy if she is at home. Honestly!!!

We cats are naturally nosey. When Monk had mentioned that the night was chess night, it immediately made us want to see what was going on. He had not asked us over, but we decided to gatecrash anyway. Charlotte declined the invitation to join us as she was not anxious to meet strange humanoids, although she was attached to Missy who was very kind to her. But Charlotte was not sure she would be greeted in the same way by those she had never met. I think the real reason was that she was completely enthralled with her new home, new cage, and tantalizing food.

Fortunately, Missy had a dinner appointment with a business client that evening and she had, as usual, given us our snack of fat free yoghurt before she took off. Fromage suggested that perhaps we would be served some goodies over at Monk's place.

"Keep dreaming," I said, and slipped out of our flap door followed by my two musketeers. *'Here we come'*, I said to myself. Dr. House (the pussy cat version!!!), and her loyal, hardworking but long suffering team consisting of Fromage, the greatest cheese monger in the world, and Cara, the gorgeous seal point.

We quietly crept up to the main house. The kitchen was in total darkness; apparently Hobbs had closed it for the night. Fromage said, "Terrance told me that he and Hobbs were going down to the pub tonight since Solo has company. Hobbs tends to fall asleep watching Solo and Inspector Reid play chess. Since he snores, Solo has banned him from the library when a chess session was on. Terrance says that Hobbs is more of an action man and he is the brawn behind the brains team of Solo and Company. But Monk refutes this claim saying, "Solo is not only the brains behind the outfit but also the brawn." Well, well, nothing like sibling rivalry to keep the home fires burning, I thought.

"All this hardly matters, let's get going," I said. We crept through Monk and Terrance's flap in to the kitchen.

Fromage, seeing the place deserted, said, "Wait a minute, now that the coast is clear, let's take a look at the pantry. Sure to be interesting."

"Fromage," I shushed. "No way are we going to investigate our neighbor's pantry uninvited. You are asking for trouble; if they catch us, they will report to Missy."

"No shame, no gain," muttered Fromage, nevertheless falling into step behind me.

The great hall, the huge dining room and the downstairs were bathed in a warm glow, except for the kitchen and pantry area that were dark and still. The big house smelt of warm oak and floor polish; it was spotless as usual. Monk had told us that Hobbs supervised a group of cleaners who come in weekly to maintain the house in its immaculate condition. But there was no one around. "They should be in the library," I said and led the way to the library.

We peeped at the open doorway of the library. All was quiet but seated, where we normally sat when we had our midnight 'pow-wows', were two gentlemen deep in concentration over the chess board. Monk was sitting perched on the arm of the leather sofa of one of the gentlemen, and my guess was this was Solo. He was staring fixedly at the chess board too. What was this fascination with this little checkered board? I had to get to the bottom of this.

We watched silently from behind a large sofa. Nobody moved. What were we supposed to do, just watch them bent over the board deep in thought? No way.

I said, "Let's go and introduce ourselves. Come on!" I padded over leading the way with the other two close behind and gently rubbed my head on Solo's ankles.

Solo looked down surprised! "Who is this?" said Solo, scooping me up in his arms. He observed me closely and said, "Light as a feather." I tilted my head to a side and looked at him carefully. "Now I understand what Ambrose Brown meant when he said, 'The cat has been described as the most perfect animal, the acme of muscular perfection and the supreme example in the animal kingdom of the coordination of mind and muscle'," said Solo, looking at me.
I purred back to him in return, "The mind of God may be glimpsed in the eyes of a cat, so say the Celts, *Mon Ami.*"

Solo was tall, athletically built with deep set black eyes and black hair slightly long and tussled. He was neatly dressed in a casual suit. From Monk's goings on about him, I knew that Solo loved books and music and had a large collection of both.

Apparently he was friendly but had an introverted personality, cherishing his independence and solitude. According to Monk, Solo was the perfect companion for him. They both valued their serenity, preferring neither restless children nor too much noise with the exception of jazz which they both adored. Solo's one true friend dating back to his university days in Oxford was Inspector Reid. They both had a lot in common being interested in solving crimes of all sorts.

According to Monk, Solo had repeatedly given his discrete services to many of the royal houses of Europe on sensitive matters that they did not wish to become public. Sometimes they came to him instead of the police as he was able to solve many cases in a subtle manner, keeping them away from the nosy press. Hence his reputation had spread by word of mouth amongst the upper circles as one who could be trusted to be discrete in handling cases.

Inspector Reid, like his friend, was tall and lanky but with sandy brown hair; he was addicted to his pipe which he had clumped between his teeth. He rarely smiled and looked stern and solemn, but I understood from Monk that, despite his stern appearance, he was kind, good and attached to Solo, Monk and Terrance, not to mention Hobbs. Both Solo and Inspector Reid were in their late thirties.

Inspector Reid had picked up Cara and was examining her as if she was a clinical specimen. Cara kept looking at me as if to confirm that it was alright to be carried by a complete stranger.

"Interesting," said Solo as he looked at the three of us. "These must be our new neighbors. I remember having dinner with Florence before she left when she told me about the three furry friends who would be my immediate neighbors. This must be Inca"

"I understand from Florence that Siberians generally have an affectionate temperament, a number of dog-like characteristics, high intelligence and the capacity of excellent problem solving skills," said Solo. *What?* I thought, and I was under the impression that I was the only one who was so intelligent!

"Let me get some goodies for them from the kitchen. After all, we should be hospitable, right, old man?" Solo said to Monk and strode into the kitchen, dropping me gently by Monk. He left the library making his way swiftly and lightly to the pantry with long and swinging strides. Solo was finely built and in his younger days had represented his university and country football matches, retaining an impressive record. He still kept himself in good form and was quick and light on his feet. I had the impression that he was strong, even though he was slightly built.

He returned with some food belonging to Monk on a plate with cream in a large dish. We tasted the goodies he set before us with appreciative eyes. It is true that we had already had our evening supper set out by Missy, but there was always room for seconds. Missy worries that we may put on weight and is careful to cook most of our meals from scratch, generally consisting of fresh fish steamed or cooked. But what she does not know will not harm her, I thought.

"He is kind," said Fromage, smacking his lips and starting to clean himself. Fromage, being Fromage, had managed to eat the major portion of the food served to us by Solo. Cara watched us with disapproval, her blue eyes accusing us of being disloyal to Missy.

She whispered to me, "No wonder Monk has a portly air about him. Imagine eating cream in such quantities." *Honestly*, I thought to myself, what a prissy Cara can be at times.

"Let's take a break," Inspector Reid said. "It's not often that we have guests." Solo chuckled, went over to the music system and put on some music. The large library swelled with music which had an underlying pulse that made us wish to tap our paws to its beat. Fromage was enchanted as he never was before by the salsa music that moved me. He couldn't control himself and started twisting his tail and wagging his bottom, rocking to the tempo. Reid and Solo started laughing; even Reid's doleful countenance had relaxed.

"What music is this?" I asked Monk.

"That's my namesake, Thelonious Monk, playing his jazz music. Solo actually named me after him. He is not a bad jazz musician, but my preferred artist is Louis Armstrong and I still regret that Solo did not name me after him. I would have made a spiffy Louis, don't you think?" Monk suddenly jumped and went to the music center and fiddled with the knobs. As he did that, the library was filled with a raspy velvet voice crooning, *'What a wonderful world'*.

I was flabbergasted. Not only does Monk know how to open doors, but he also knows how to change music on Solo's music player and Solo lets him do that? "Cool," said Fromage. Missy never allows us to go near the television set or the music center. While it is true that Fromage is a clumsy clot, what about me? Surely I could do that too. I thought to myself that I should try when Missy was not at home and when the others were not looking in case I failed. I would probably need some practice and didn't wish to look a complete clot in front of the others. I had my reputation as *'chief lady Inca felicitus'* to maintain after all.

At that moment, Terrance walked in with a humanoid. Monk said, "Here comes Hobbs, you have not met him before, have you?"

Hobbs was a tall and upright person in his early forties with a sleek head of black hair pasted to his scalp. Monk had informed us that Hobbs was part of the family and his father had been in the service of Solo senior like Missy's uncle Norman's grandfather who had inherited our present cottage for his long and faithful years of service. Solo's father had made Hobbs a well-educated man and he was the devoted and trustworthy right-hand man to Solo. Not only was he responsible for Solo's large house, ensuring that it was run to perfection, but he also aided Solo in his cases. Hobbs was Solo's loyal bodyguard, accompanying him around the globe on his adventures. Hobbs, like Solo, had studied martial arts, both earning black belts and had experience and connections with the criminal underworld; he often assisted Solo through his numerous contacts. Terrance was his well-trained dog and best mate of Monk.

Hobbs gave the impression that he floated when he walked. He gave a kindly eye to the gathering in the library and seemed pleased to meet us. He said, "Family members of Florence, I presume," in a smooth, plummy voice.

Soon after, Monk asked, "Inca, I am going to see Polo. Do you want to come with me?"

"Yes, we all do," I said. "I want to introduce Polo to Cara and Charlotte. They have never met him." So getting Missy's troupe together, with Charlotte in her usual place on Fromage's neck, we crept through the hole in the thick hedge and went over to Polo's house. He was not visible and Monk crept quietly while we stayed near the hole to see where Polo was. Monk jumped on the kitchen window to see if Polo was in the kitchen and entered the house. He came out after five minutes and asked us to join him. We all leapt onto the window and cautiously entered the silent house, avoiding the flap door which Monk claimed made a small sound, unlike his.

Polo was in the kitchen waiting to meet us. Monk had found him in the grand hall with his head on his paws contemplating the sad sorry status of his beloved *Señora*. After introducing Cara to Polo and they greeting each other, Monk asked him where the *Señora* was.

"She is taking a nap after having a light lunch but Banks is in the garage cleaning the car, so please quiet everyone," Polo cautioned.

"Any new development on your side, Polo?" Monk asked "Nothing very much other than that the *Señora* is not keeping well at all. I am very worried about her. The doctor visited yesterday and she is heavily drugged most of the time," Polo replied.

Cara and Fromage continued to talk to Polo and cheer him up. Introductions to Charlotte had been made and the sight of Charlotte seemed to brighten Polo. He had met another new friend, a charming little thing at that. I noticed that Charlotte's cute twitching nose and sympathetic appearance had this effect on those who met her.

I was pleased that Charlotte had been readily accepted not only by our doggy friends, but also by Monk. It was actually quite a relief on my side as I had been nervous about the meeting with Monk, despite what he had said to Fromage. Cats have a natural tendency to hunt rodents and, however cute or well-dressed Charlotte was, she still fitted in this category.

What surprised me was the instant empathy that developed between Charlotte and Polo. He had immediately cheered up when he met her and was chatting with her like an old friend, telling her about all his woes. I will say this for Charlotte, she is a very good listener. I guess she has ample experience after listening to our garrulous Fromage. Polo invited her over whenever she wished. Despite the refusal of my invitation, given his need to be near the *Señora*, Polo promised to come over to see Charlotte when we were away in the store in case she was lonely. That was nice of Polo.

Charlotte and her new friend Polo

But this sudden attraction between Charlotte and Polo was not as well received by our Fromage who developed a sudden scowl. I heard him telling Charlotte, "Charlotte, I don't think it's a good idea for you to be roaming about alone." Charlotte's nose twitched rapidly, surprised by Fromage's sudden change in demeanor. What was going on? I suddenly realized that the green-eyed monster had taken over Fromage's usually kind heart and that he was jealous of this new friendship. He was used to having Charlotte's undivided attention and to be suddenly usurped by a rival was not to his liking. Did I hear him muttering to Charlotte that we French must stick together? I couldn't believe my ears. I had to take him to a corner and give him a good talking to.

All was forgotten, however, when we heard the telephone ringing outside and Monk went to see whose telephone it was. I padded after him. When we peeped into the garage we found Banks in a white T-shirt talking on the phone. We heard him saying, "Yes, I will open the door for you now. Everything is back to normal; *Señora* is heavily drugged so she will not need me anymore."

When he turned around, I could see him smiling. Monk whispered, "Let's get out of here before he sees us." We ran back to Polo.

Monk asked Polo, "Does Banks have a friend who visits?"

"That's Polly, she works as *Señora*'s manicurist and visits often. Banks became friendly with her a few months ago. She is friendly and a chatterbox, but *Señora* considers her somewhat of a dimwit and easily led by foolish talk," Polo explained.

We hid under the cloth on the large table in the kitchen when Banks opened the back door for Polly. Polly had a bold and challenging beauty about her. She had bright red hair, large ruby red lips and bold eyes that were sparkling and bright. I looked deeply at her from underneath the table cloth. She had an infectious giggle and seemed to be bursting with goodwill, at least for Banks. But, though a pleasing spectacle, she seemed to me like one of those girls who looked to be always having a good time and not very sensible. However, I could understand why Polo liked her as she

122

tickled him under the chin and said, "Hi, my little polo" while Banks hustled her into his quarters.

I heard Monk whispering to Polo that he would come over the following night at the same time just to check on him. My eyes shone, was he planning on snooping on Banks? He was not going to be one up on me. I was determined to sneak out, leaving the rest of the gang at home to see what Monk was up to.

Chapter 6
Grand opening!

The next morning was D-day for Fromage & Associates. There was a feeling of expectation and excitement at home.

We left bright and early with Missy for the shop, leaving Charlotte behind in charge of the cottage. When we arrived we found the shop in mint condition. The shop logo installed above the entrance showed our Fromage holding a baguette in one hand before a table covered with a checked cloth which was laden with different types of French cheese. He had his usual impish cheeky look with his brand new beret pulled down over one ear as usual and his Parisian scarf floating in the wind. When Fromage saw himself for the first time framed above the entrance, I could see that he was very pleased. I saw him visibly growing in stature and Cara and I exchanged discreet smiles unknown to him. But we were both pleased for him – after all, he was our bratty, lovable kid brother.

The small tables in the café area had checked tablecloths and the menus had Fromage on the cover. Even the tea and coffee mugs had his face on them. As a special incentive to attract crowds, the first 100 customers who bought cheese on the opening day were to be offered a delicious cheese croissant free of charge.

The supplement in the newspaper had been published the previous day and we were pleased to see how nice we all looked. There was a long article mentioning the kinds of cheese that would be on sale and what was being offered. Missy had revealed the proposition to the first 100 customers – a delicious croissant, if they purchased our cheese. So the smell of fresh croissants and bread filled the shop; it was aromatic and mouthwatering.

Fromage was beside himself with exhilaration and pride. He strutted around like a little peacock eyeing everything and checking the place out as if he was the super master of catering services. We followed him as he excitedly spoke to us, "Look at how perfectly the different kinds of cheese are arranged. Jacques and Genevieve have done a good job with the croissants and baguettes. The ripe cheese looks scrumptious doesn't it, gals? Perhaps they should be arranged a bit differently? What do you 'gals' think? I wish Charlotte was with us now, she has a good eye for arranging cheese."

I assured him that it all looked very appetizing and the place looked perfect. Cara added, "Fromage, you forgot to mention Missy's contribution. I think everything looks so perfect because of Missy's golden touch."

"Of course," said Fromage. "Missy is our wonder-mum, she has me to guide and inspire her, after all. Let's go upstairs and check out the kitchen." We followed him, shaking our heads. What else would we expect from him?

The doors opened at 8am to catch the office crowd on their way to work. Wow! What a crowd! People were standing in line to buy cheese, baguettes and receive their free fresh croissant. The resemblance to a tin of sardines came to my mind as people were jammed one to another, queuing up while inhaling the fragrance of enticing hot cheese croissants in the air. Jacques was taking orders from the customers sitting at the tables and passing them to Genevieve who was busy fulfilling those orders. Missy was behind the counter cutting out cheese or completing the orders from the already wrapped cheese pieces and adding a fresh croissant to each order in the paper bags with the logo of Fromage.

Logo for the new cheese shop

Missy had placed all three of us on the top of the tall shelves. We could have jumped down easily as there was a step placed next to the shelves. Since Fromage refused to budge, we stayed put with him looking down at the customers. They in turn noticed us and seemed enthralled with us, frequently asking questions about us. Some even wanted to pet us, but Missy didn't think that was a good idea. I knew what was on Missy's mind. She was paranoid that someone would steal us. I noticed the look on her face, so I made sure the others understood that we should not give cause for Missy to worry unnecessarily.

Missy looked up at us and said, "At some time you will have to go to the basement where all your toys and paraphernalia are placed." Fromage refused to move, so we decided to keep him company. Actually, it was fascinating sitting up there, hearing the praises showered on us and watching people coming and going with bags of fresh baguettes, croissants and cheese.

Very soon all the sandwiches prepared sold out and we heard Missy say, "Please come tomorrow, but you could buy some nice French cheese and baguettes, if you wish."

Poor Jacques, Genevieve and Missy! They had been run off their feet. Around 2pm Missy had made us go to the basement where our lunch was set out. For the rest of the afternoon we stayed in the basement playing with our toys or taking a nap. Fromage watched the goings on upstairs on the four screens where you could see the shop from various angles. The shop closed at 7.30pm as scheduled. The door of the basement opened at 7.30pm and Missy asked us to come up. We bounded up the stairs.

What a day! The shelves were almost empty. Missy's idea to get us in the supplement had really paid off.

Genevieve said, "I believe Fromage, Inca and Cara were magnets in drawing the crowds." The afternoon customers kept asking if they could see the cats that were in the newspaper article. I had to inform them that they were here this morning and would from now on only come in once a week. They seemed disappointed though.

"Well Fromage can come in more often, but I prefer Inca and Cara stay at home, as we did in Avenue de la Bourdonnais," answered Missy.

Despite the brisk business, Missy was cautious. It could be the free croissants that attracted all the customers. Let's see how it goes tomorrow. Jacques said, "Missy, we cannot rest on just a first day's success. You have to start thinking on how we can get clients such as owners of restaurants and cafés interested in cheese platters."

Cara looked at me worried. "Inca, will all this work and stress be too much for Missy?"

Fromage said, "Not to worry, gals, I will help Missy. So rest assured it will all work out well, I promise."

"Hmm…I don't think I can count on Fromage alone. I need to think how I can help Missy myself." As the eldest, it was my responsibility to ensure that Missy and the others had peace of mind and that Fromage & Associates was a success.

We left after about an hour. Missy had helped Jacques and Genevieve to clean up the place and set the tables for the next day. The young couple would be up at 6am to prepare the baguettes and croissants for the day. Jacques had told Missy that if the clients kept coming in as they had on the first day; they would have to look for another hand, may be even two, to assist in the café and shop. This would liberate Missy to concentrate full time on large scale sales of cheese to restaurants and other clients.

We drove back with Missy listening to music. Missy and Fromage were both happy; she about the day's sales, and he about his new shop and cafe. Cara and I were happy because they were happy.

Missy ran a bath and we crowded into the bathroom with her to play with the water. Cats are supposed to detest water. But from day one, we have been fascinated when Missy runs her bath. We walk around the edge of the tub, play with the water pouring into the tub and sometimes take turns sipping water from the running tap. Once

Missy gets in, we sit and watch her relaxing in the water listening to soft music. The bathroom has a lovely herbal fragrance from the essence that is poured into the bathtub and the steamy hot water makes the place warm and cozy. This is another activity that Charlotte gently declined to participate in; as she put it to Fromage *"Jamais Mon Ami, pas pour moi."* We were all in bed soon after with Missy falling asleep very soon. I knew she was tired after standing on her feet the whole day.

That night, my natural inquisitive nature could not resist knowing what Monk was up to in Polo's house. Why did he wish to see him in the middle of the night by himself? He had not invited us to join him as he had done so far. My curiosity got the better of me. We couldn't all go uninvited so I decided not to mention that I had overheard Monk planning to visit Polo at midnight and went as usual to sleep with the others. Missy was generally tired these days working in the shop full time and there was less of listening to music in the evenings with us. So we were in bed by 10.00pm

Around 11.45pm, I cautiously woke up so as not to disturb the others. If I had mentioned to Fromage that I was going to Polo's to see what Monk was up to, I was sure he would wish to join me and no way could I have stopped him. Cara preferred to curl up next to Missy and not move from her warm and cozy spot, if she could help it.

I cautiously slipped out of my cot, but Fromage, who is a light sleeper, stirred and asked drowsily, "Where are you going, Inca?"

"Go back to sleep, Fromage," I said. "I just wish to take a tinkle. I will be back soon." I silently padded out of the room and swiftly ran down the stairs and out of the flap in the kitchen door. In a flash I was out of the house. It was very dark outside but there was a single light on the large porch outside Monk's house faintly lighting up part of the enormous garden. But I didn't need any light. I could see very well in the dark as my eyes had grown large and black like an X-ray beam.

I swiftly ran on the grass, still warm from the bright hot summer afternoon sun, hardly making a sound on the manicured lawn all the way to the side of the house where I knew the hole to Polo's house was. Quickly slipping through the hole, I hid behind a large urn on Polo's porch to take stock of the situation when I saw Monk's rotund but elegant figure creeping in through the hole. He ran up to Polo's kitchen. He entered through the flap as if it was his own house. He seemed to be at ease in Polo's house as if he had a habit of visiting often. I slowly went up to the window and jumped on to the sill to see what they were doing. I couldn't see anyone, neither Polo nor Monk. They were not in the kitchen. I presumed they had moved into the large dining room. The way was clear. So I jumped down from the windowsill and quietly crept into the kitchen through the flap.

Noiselessly I passed by the silent kitchen, noticing that the pantry door was open and the large ball of cheese was still uncut on top of the shelf. The cut piece that Fromage had eyed but could not get at due to it being under a heavy glass cover had disappeared. I guess eaten up by the *Señora* and Banks since we last saw it. Not paying much attention to the pantry, I entered the large silent dining room and still no Monk and Polo. Where could they have gone, I wondered? I felt like quietly turning around and rushing back home to my warm cot and my family. However, my curiosity was not yet satisfied and I wished to see what the two were up to. Where were they? What were they doing? Sometimes my inquisitiveness gets the better of me.

I went past the silent dining room into the great hall and still no sign of them. They probably went upstairs, I thought, and slowly started climbing the stairs. I peeked into the first bedroom on the landing but there was no one there. Suddenly, I heard singing and the playing of the piano. The music was coming from the *Señora's* sitting room. I knew from my previous visit that the *Señora* had a large sitting room with piano, comfortable armchairs in printed tissue, with a small dining room attached where she usually had her meals. She never came downstairs either to the kitchen or used the large dining room unless she had guests. But she had not invited anyone for a meal for a very long time, according to Polo.

I couldn't contain my curiosity anymore and cautiously put my head in through the door to see what was going on. Surprise! It was the *Señora* sitting on a piano stool singing in a low beautiful soprano voice. Polo was looking at his mistress with adoring eyes and Monk? What was Monk doing? Yes, he was sitting on top of the piano gazing into the *Señora'* s eyes. It was as if the *Señora* was singing the melodious song only to him. This was a welcome surprise since Polo had mournfully told us that the *Señora* had stopped singing for some time now. She loved to sing so he had known that she was really sad and depressed.

No one had noticed my silent entry so I noiselessly padded over to the *Señora* and brushed against her legs. She looked down at me. She looked surprised and then gently started laughing. Even her laughter was soft and musical. "Who is this pretty little lady, Polo? Is she a friend of yours or Monk's? When did you become friends? Why have I not seen her before?"

I jumped on her lap and gently rubbed my face against her face and gave her one of my most appealing looks, my large eyes shining, my head turned slightly to the side. The look I reserve for newcomers; the look I am aware most humans cannot resist. I have been able to entice even the hardest hearted cat hater with this appealing posture. *Señora* genuinely liked cats and dogs so conquering her was no great feat. I knew she was smitten. She gently stroked my head and whispered endearments into my ear. Yes, another conquest.

I looked deep into her eyes to see what was going on in her mind. I held my breath when I saw deep shadows of sadness and much pain clouding her mind, taking me back to Marie-France, my first companion. Marie-France had travelled from Paris to La Celle St-Cloud, a beautiful little village close to Versailles, where the famous Chateau de Versailles is located, to collect me from my breeder. She paid a tidy sum of 1000 Euros for the privilege of my companionship. We had settled down well enough since I have a very amenable nature ready to open my heart to my humanoid.

Señora is smitten! What else?

We had lived together for just three months when disaster struck. Marie-France's mother passed away unexpectedly. Her father, who had been married to Marie-France's mother for 40 years, could not bear the separation and decided to leave this world on his own by walloping a whole bottle of sleeping pills with his evening mug of hot chocolate. Marie-France rushed him to hospital and stayed by his side day and night coming home only to feed me. It was a difficult time for the both of us. I was very young and felt terribly alone. I could see, reading Marie-France, that she was not well at all; herself incapable of anything other than worrying about her father and grappling with her loss of her mother. I had tried my best to comfort her but I knew it was not possible. All she wanted was to sit beside her father who was lying on the hospital bed, still as a piece of wood while Marie-France kept on urgently whispering to him not to abandon this world.

Marie-France was going to pieces before my eyes as she could not cope with life. It was at that time that she asked the guardian of our building if there was anyone who could take over looking after me. I knew instinctively that Marie-France needed my psychological and moral support and tried to spend time with her. But she was rarely at home and when she was, she locked herself into the bed room leaving me outside alone. I had a heavy heart wondering what would become of me.

Missy had heard about this misfortune and came to visit us as the guardian spoke to her about Marie-France and the need for her to find someone to take me. I have imprinted in my head the glorious evening Missy paid a visit to Marie-France. As usual, the moment the doorbell rang I had charged to the door to see who was visiting us. Missy looked at me and I looked at her and it was as if time stood still. I had the illusion of having been struck by lightning. I guess this is what is termed *love at first sight*. It happens like this sometimes. One recognizes instantly one's soul mate. Bright stars circle overhead, making one realize that this is it. Love that requires long months before it comes to fruition can sometimes develop instantaneously like an explosion that blows people to small pieces. That very evening I said goodbye to Marie-France and Missy carried me down to her apartment. I doubt it even registered with Marie-France that I was leaving.

It is as if Missy and I were meant to be. So I have no regrets, but I do understand pain and grief in others. Subsequently, I heard from Missy that Marie-France had picked up the pieces and returned to normality. As far as Marie-France was concerned, she had moved on, and she needed a fresh start. Thus, she never asked me to come back, thankfully; since Missy and I were so happy together it would have broken both our hearts if we had to be parted.

Thoughts of Marie-France flooded my mind when I looked into *Señora's* mind. But as I went on looking into her sad mental state, I saw a sudden spark of interest in me, Monk, and a lot of love for

Polo hidden deep down clouded by her sadness. I tried to convey Polo's love for her by sending waves of love to her from Polo telepathically and how sad he was that she was locking herself out of his life. I kept on repeating the telepathic waves between the *Señora* and me, "Polo loves you, Polo needs you." I was hoping that I got through to her since I had so far practiced my powers mainly on Missy and I was not sure if my influence extended to the *Señora*.

However, my fears were soon abated. The *Señora* said to Polo, "My little Polo, I know you have been sad that I have been so withdrawn. I promise to try very hard to get back to normal soon. Let's start tomorrow by going to the park like we used to. How would you like that?"

Polo was beside himself with happiness and he excitedly jumped around her licking her face. The *Señora* laughed again. *'What a nice laugh she has'*, I thought. *'I have to ask her to come around to meet Missy'*. So once again, before she could get up from the seat, I quickly looked deep into her eyes and conveyed the message that she should come and introduce herself to Missy.

As if by magic, the *Señora* said, "I will come next door, little one, I imagine you just moved into the cottage where Florence lived. Florence is my good friend and I was sad that she moved away. She did tell me her niece was coming from Paris to start a cheese shop in London and that she was bringing her three lovely cats with her. It's just that I have been so out of sorts these last months that I have even neglected my loyal Polo. But I promise I will drop by soon to say hello. I know your mistress tried to telephone me and had left several messages, but I just could not talk to anyone. I will come around and apologize."

Looking at her kind gentle face, I suddenly had a great fear. How I hope that she hadn't taken the necklace and pretended that someone else had stolen it. How awful that would be. She was so sweet and kind. Imagine what Polo would feel. He would be devastated, so ashamed and scared if his mistress was taken in by the police. The situation would be more distressing than I had imagined previously now that I had met the *Señora*.

Suddenly we heard a great big crash downstairs. The crash shook the house and after a few minutes we heard a loud and long yowl…. I jumped nervously and Polo went rushing out yapping in his high pitched bark. Monk ran after him to see what had happened and the *Señora* took me in her arms and slowly followed with frightened eyes.

"Polo," she whispered. "Wait, should I call the police? Where is Banks? Didn't he hear the noise? Did he lock the door when he went to sleep?"

"Should I call the police?" she muttered in my ear again.

I leapt out of her arms as I suddenly recognized that noise. It was no human voice but a loud yowl of a cat. That was my brother, Fromage. I recognized that yowl. He must have sounded exactly like that when Jacques pulled him out of the fondant pot in the basement of our shop on Avenue de la Bourdonnais. Fromage has quite a frightening yowl as witnessed by both Jacques and Genevieve who never get tired of relating the story of Fromage and the fondant pot to us.

I ran like a bullet let out by a mad cowboy completely alarmed. What on earth could have made Fromage yell like that? Surely there were no fondant urns in the *Señora's* house.

The noise had come from downstairs near the kitchen. Through the open pantry door, we saw that the great cheese was on the floor split into several pieces. I guess the fall had made it break into pieces. The noise was due to the glass plate crashing to the floor with the cheese and shattering into thousand pieces.

Oh la! What a disaster. I heard the *Señora* say, *"Ay, Caramba!* What happened here?"

Then I saw Cara crouched under the table trembling. Tears were rolling down from her large eyes, the irises had turned midnight blue. She looked frightened and upset. Where was Fromage? I know that she would not have had the nerve to investigate the cheese resulting in the broken plate and destroyed cheese. This was Fromage's handy work to be sure.

At that moment Banks came out of his room yawning as if he had just got up and said to the *Señora,* "What is going on *Señora;* where did all these cats come from? What a mess they have made! Look at our beautiful cheese, *Señora.* I was maturing it for your Christmas dinner, but it has been destroyed. Let me throw these cats out. Monk must have brought them over. I told you repeatedly that no good would come from letting Monk come in here and become friends with Polo. He could only bring about trouble."

This is the first time I had seen Banks up close. He was a large bull-like man in his early thirties. I didn't like the look of him. He looked strong like a former boxer with a close shaved head. I had heard from Polo that he had actually been a bodyguard to the *Señora*'s wealthy husband. When he passed away to the other world after the accident, Banks had offered to stay on and become a chauffeur and house man for the *Señora.* Since she was in such a sad state of mind and Banks already knew the house very well, she had agreed to this proposition. Her own cook had left at that point and the arrangement had seemed the easiest solution for the tired and sad *Señora.*

The *Señora* said, "What nonsense, Banks. It is only cheese after all. I am not a cheese fan anyway and certainly would feel no loss at not having it served for my Christmas supper. I am happy that Polo has found lots of new friends. You know that they live next door and belong to the niece of my good friend, Florence. Please stop making a fuss and clean up this mess."

Banks gave us a scowl, his face red and angry, but without a word he started cleaning up the broken pottery and cheese. We knew that if the *Señora* had not been present, he would have come at us with the large broom in his hands.

"Polo, it is time we all went to bed," the *Señora* continued. "Say goodnight to your friends. I will open the kitchen door so that they can all leave that way to their homes." She looked at me as I was leaving and said, "I will visit your mistress soon, pretty one. Thank you for visiting."

Monk, Cara and I went outside. "That was a close call," said Monk. Cara slouched besides me trying her best to make herself invisible.

She was still crying and I licked her face saying, "Cara, it's alright. I am here. What happened, why are you crying? I know it's not good to have the cheese on the floor but there is no need to cry; please stop crying. What are you doing here? Did you come by yourself? You know Missy and I don't like you running about by yourself without Fromage or me."

Cara was so upset she was shaking. "It looks serious," said Monk. "Cara, please stop crying and explain to us what happened. Tell us quickly as we need to know what happened urgently."

Cara swallowed hard and stopped crying and said, "Inca, when you didn't come back from your tinkle, Fromage got worried and wanted to go searching for you. I was worried too and decided to come with him. Fromage wouldn't allow Charlotte to join us though and ordered her back to her cot when she tried to climb into his scarf." I could imagine very well why, I thought. He didn't want to give her another chance to meet Polo. This was Fromage at his stupidest.

"We thought you may have gone to see Monk so we went to the great house and into the library but Monk was not there. Terrance was sleeping in front of the fireplace which was not burning as it is so hot this summer," Cara said.

"Terrance told us that Monk had gone to see the *Señora* and Polo and so we thought the only place you could be was at Polo's too." She looked at me reproachfully as if to say *'why didn't you tell us'* but continued quickly, hardly pausing for breath.

"We came over here and entered through the flap door. As we were passing the pantry, Fromage spotted the cheese. He couldn't resist it and was greatly tempted to see how English cheese tasted as compared to French cheese. I begged him not to jump on the shelf in someone else's house and eat food uninvited, but he would not listen. He kept saying, *'Cara, you have to understand that I am a professional cheese monger. How would it look to my fellow cheese mongers if I did not taste a new cheese?'* So I stayed hidden behind a stool and he jumped on the shelf to sniff at the cheese before tasting it."

"He was keen to take a bite of the cheese. He investigated the large cheese and found a soft spot on top and dug his paw in it. He scooped out a bit or, should I say, quite a large piece. He tasted it smacking his lips as he normally does whenever he is introduced to a new cheese and said, *'Not bad, not bad at all'.* As if that was not enough, much to my distress, he said, *'Let me taste a little bit more, the first time was for taste but the second piece will be to test for quality'.*

"You know how he is when it comes to cheese. He is also quite clumsy. He kept pushing with his nose to get a better grip and to go deeper down the middle of the cheese. He pushed too far and the great cheese crashed to the ground with Fromage on top of it. There was a loud clatter and the large ceramic plate on which the cheese had rested was broken into smithereens. Fromage descended in a shower of cheese and something gleaming entangled around his neck. He shook his head and complained, *'It's not my fault; there was really nothing to hold on to'.* I told him that he had made a mess of it. But Fromage just shook himself again philosophically saying, *'We cheese mongers have to suffer for our trade'."*

"But then something bad happened. Banks rushed out of his room at the noise and went completely crazy. He picked Fromage up by the back of his neck. The sparkling necklace was still entangled around Fromage's neck. He grabbed the necklace from Fromage's neck, put it in his pajama trouser pocket, ran to the front door, opened it, and threw Fromage out. That's when Fromage let out a loud yowl."

Monk and I looked at each other. I thought to myself, *'So that's where Banks, or was it the Señora, had hidden the diamond necklace'.* Surely it couldn't have been the *Señora.* I felt relieved. No, it was Banks who cooked and served the meals for Polo and the *Señora.* Polo had talked about being fed by Banks in the kitchen. The *Señora* ate upstairs in her little dining room unless she had guests. From Polo's conversation, I knew that she had stopped entertaining anyone since Raoul passed away. But what about Fromage? And where was he now?

Monk looked worried. "That door leads out into the street."

My heart sank. Why, oh why did I come here, leaving them alone? If I had not ventured out, they wouldn't have followed me and Fromage would not be in this situation, lost perhaps forever. I knew that gentle Cara had no influence on preventing him doing something naughty. He would only listen to Missy or me when he was in his mischievous mood.

Fromage had never ventured out of the compound other than in Missy's car. He was a French cat just arrived in London. Even though we lived in a residential area, he did not know the place. Where would he have gone? He must have been so frightened when Banks roughly threw him out of the door, even though being a cat he would have fallen on his feet. Cats normally have nine lives, but I knew in the case of Fromage, one of those lives had already been lost with his fall into the fondant pot.

My mind went numb. I guess Monk saw the look of fear and horror in my eyes. He said, "Cara, are you sure that Banks took the necklace and went into his room? He didn't put it anywhere else did he?"

"No I am sure of that," said Cara. "He didn't see me, but I definitely saw him. He pulled the necklace out of Fromage's neck very roughly, slipped it into his pajama trouser pocket and rushed to the front door, opening it with one hand and throwing Fromage out with the other. He then rushed back to his room and closed the door. He only came out when you all and the *Señora* came downstairs, pretending to have been asleep."

It suddenly occurred to me. Goodness! What would Missy say? She would be so upset if anything happened to Fromage. I turned to Monk, "What shall we do?"

Monk said, "Wait a minute, Inca; we must act rationally and quickly. I am going to get Terrance and wake up Solo. You have to go to Missy; tell her everything, about Fromage and the necklace, and bring her quickly over to Solo's house." So Monk knew about my telepathic powers. Fromage had blabbed about that too.

"Terrance and Solo should go looking for Fromage and Missy must go with them. Cara should hide behind this urn in the porch and wait here for us to come back without moving. She should keep her eyes open to see if Banks tries to go out this way. For the moment, I believe he thinks he is safe, but I don't know how long it will be before he makes a move."

"Cara, don't be frightened," I whispered to her. "I will be back very soon. But you have to stay here hidden so no one will know you are here." She looked at me with frightened eyes but nodded her head in agreement. Monk and I ran fast to the hole and crept to our side of the house. I ran to our cottage and he ran to his house eager to wake up Terrance first, and then Solo.

I sprinted in to our cottage and flew up the stairs to sleeping Missy. There was no time for gentle wake up techniques. I jumped on her and sat on her chest with a thump. She woke up with a start and quickly reached for the bedside lamp and turned on the light.

She said, "Inca, what is wrong? I have never seen you like this before, what is going on?" I quickly caught her eyes and started sending telepathic waves into her mind as rapidly as I could. I have never done it so fast before. I kept repeating, "Fromage found the diamond necklace inside *Senora's* cheese ball and Banks has thrown Fromage out on the street and pocketed the necklace." I think I repeated this same statement at least 15 times, urgently going faster and faster each time I repeated it. I had not muttered a word and only spoken to Missy through telepathy. I had done that because I didn't want Charlotte to know what was going on. I couldn't deal with another panicked family member. I knew Charlotte would be distraught if she knew something had happened to Fromage. Despite her recent annoyance at him for his unreasonable clumsiness, I knew how attached she was to him.

I had never seen Missy move so quickly before. She grabbed a sweater, put her slippers on and ran with me at her heels to Solo's house. She started ringing the back door and pounding on the door when a startled Solo opened the door.

Monk had already woken up Terrance and they had dashed into Solo's bedroom. Terrance had started barking sharply and pulling Solo's covers from him and onto the floor. Monk had jumped on Solo's stomach. Between the two of them, Solo was wide awake and calling to Hobbs. They had worked with Terrance long enough to know that Terrance had some important news to tell them.

At that moment, Missy started pounding on the door and Solo opened the door and looked at her amazed with Hobbs behind him. That was the first time they had met since we arrived in London. The last time they had met was nearly 15 years ago and both of them were both very young. But he remembered her instantly as she did him.

"No time for introductions," said the agitated Missy with me behind her. "My cat, Fromage, found the diamond necklace buried in a cheese in the *Señora*'s house and Banks has it with him in his room and he has thrown Fromage onto the streets. You have to help me find Fromage quickly. He has never been out of the compound and he must be lonely and frightened. Please, please help us," said Missy bursting into tears.

Solo, the super detective, lived up to his reputation. He quickly turned around to Hobbs and told him, "Hobbs, phone Inspector Reid immediately and tell him that we were right. It is Banks who has stolen the necklace. He has it with him now. He should call for reinforcements since he should catch Banks with the necklace on him. While he is coming, take the Land Rover and park it across the *Señora*'s garage door so that in case Banks tries to escape, he will not be able to do so by car which should slow him down somewhat. I will go with Terrance and Missy to look for Fromage. Monk, you and this little cat should go over to the *Señora*'s house and keep an eye out to see if Banks tries to leave."

I had told Missy that Cara was safe and she should concentrate on Fromage. So she ran out of the door with Terrance and Solo. She was clearly upset; as I was. Our Fromage, all alone on the streets of

London! My only hope was that he landed on his feet and was wise enough to be hiding along the street and not venturing out too far.

Knowing that Cara would be getting nervous by herself, I ran over to Polo's house with Monk close behind. I need not have worried unnecessarily about Cara. Polo had come out through the flap and had found her. They were sitting very close together waiting for us to get back. We told them of what had happened and how Hobbs had been requested by Solo to call Inspector Reid. Cara told me, "Missy will find Fromage, Inca; I know she will." Cara has confidence in Missy to save the world.

Polo said, "The *Señora* went to bed and Banks is in his room. The lights are switched off, so I am hoping that he is sleeping now."

My heart was beating and I was very anxious about Fromage. Our Fromage is a bit clumsy, as you can see from the Banks' cheese episode. He also can be a bit of a bore when he starts on his French cheese. But he was our lovable ball of fur and both Cara and I love him. What about Charlotte? She had left Paris to be close to Fromage, I didn't want to think how Charlotte would react if Fromage did not come back home. If anything happened to him, Missy would be inconsolable as we would. He is our mascot!

My heart was sinking and I felt truly miserable. Cara, sensing my distress, couldn't stop the tears pouring down her little face and both Monk and Polo looked distracted. Polo said, "Let's go in the house and you three hide under the kitchen table. The table cloth is so long that Banks will not see that you are there. It would be normal for me to be in the kitchen, so I will sit near the table. From the kitchen we can see the corridor leading to Banks room. If he comes out we can see him instantly but, since all three of you will be hiding under the table, he will not see you."

We crept into the kitchen. There was no light in there and all was dark. It was Polo's territory so he had no problems moving about in the dark. As cats, Monk, Cara and I thrive in the darkness and see most clearly when it is black.

Cara huddled against me and I kept licking her face and ears, trying to still her pounding heart. I knew that witnessing Banks brutally throw Fromage out of the house was continuously resonating in her head. We had all lived a very sheltered life with Missy. We had never experienced any one hitting us, kicking us or even abusing or shouting at us. For a little cat like Cara, this was a rude awakening to the nastiness that existed in the world.

Will I ever forget that terrible night watch? All was silent just like a tomb. I could not hear a sound, not even the breathing of my furry friends. We remained noiseless in the darkness. From outside came the occasional cry of a night bird, and once the hoot of an owl. The night continued long and still and we waited silently for whatever might transpire.

We suddenly saw a sliver of light through the bottom of Banks' door. Cara moved closer to me and I looked at Monk. "Stay quiet," whispered Monk. "Don't make a sound or move." Polo's ears had popped up as the light came on, and we held our breath wondering if Banks would step out.

Slowly the door opened and he stood at his door as if to make sure no one was around. To his knowledge, the only person in the house was the *Señora* and she never came down to the kitchen. Her meals were always served to her in her small sitting room upstairs. The great hall, large living room and even larger dining hall had not been used for months. The *Señora* never came downstairs, but I guess after the cheese episode, Banks wanted to be sure. We saw that he had a small bag in his hand. It looked as if he had decided to do a bunk or wanted to leave the house to find a safer place for the valuable diamond necklace that had been well hidden in the large round cheese in the pantry until Fromage upset the safe hiding place.

He obviously did not want to be caught with it on him, just in case the police came back to search. He had been pretty confident when they last came and searched the house. He had been cooking in the kitchen and casually moving in and out of the pantry. Even though two police constables had done a thorough job searching the kitchen, pantry, his room and the whole house, they never suspected for once that the necklace was tucked away in the middle of the big cheese sitting out in the open and visible for anyone passing by the pantry as the door was left widely open. Actually, on reflection, Banks had made a shrewd calculation that no one would suspect that the valuable necklace was lying on the pantry shelf, well hidden from the human eye.

He quietly opened the kitchen door which led to the wide back garden and garage. Solo's thinking had been correct. Banks had no intention to walk at this time of the night. He was intending to take the *Señora*'s car which he considered his as only he had been driving it since he came to work there. He was always tinkering with the car. So he knew it was in perfect condition and that he would not make a sound when it left the garage and out into the street on the other side of the house. He could be away and back and no one would be any the wiser. We watched him leaving, all of us anxiously hoping that Hobbs had parked Solo's big Land Rover across the entrance to prevent Banks from driving out and that the policemen were outside waiting to catch him.

It was pitch darkness outside and I couldn't stop blaming myself. It was now coming close to 1am in the morning, almost one hour since Banks threw Fromage out of the door. I could kick myself for having got us into this situation. I should have guessed that Fromage would never stay quietly in the cot if he suspected I had gone out. What an idiot I had been.

After Banks left, the four of us quickly came out of Polo's flap door and watched from the edge of the hedge. We held our breath and all four of us gave a sigh of relief when we heard Banks cursing. Hobbs had parked exactly across the entrance as requested by Solo and there was no way for Banks to drive past even if he rammed Solo's car.

We saw Banks leap out of the car and come charging towards us. I think his idea was to run out of the back door at the end of the garden close to our cottage into the alley and make a getaway that way. There were many large houses that he could disappear into and hide. Monk suddenly came to life. I guess he thought, as I had, that Banks was trying to get away through the back alley. Monk charged after Banks and suddenly hurled himself in front of him. I held my breath! It was so dark that Banks didn't see him, although Monk, with his cat eyes, saw perfectly well in the dark. Banks stumbled over Monk and crashed to the ground letting out an angry oath. Monk had his revenge at last, I thought! Polo barked, "Monk always gets his man."

We heard voices and the rushing of several feet. It was Hobbs with the police constables alerted by Inspector Reid and the good inspector himself.

Well done, Monk," said Inspector Reid as the two constables grabbed Banks, handcuffing him. Though it was dark, from the rays of his flashlight, Inspector Reid had seen what Monk had just done to stop Banks from getting away. He said, "Solo will be very proud of you, Monk old chap."

They soon drove Banks away in the police car. All was quite in a matter of minutes. It had all taken just 10 minutes to handcuff Banks and put him in the police car.

The *Señora* slept on undisturbed. Polo told us that she generally took a strong sleeping medication when she went to sleep. So probably she would wake up only in the morning.

Polo's case had been solved and Monk was a hero even in my eyes. My concern was still about Fromage. What had happened to the others? Where were they?

Chapter 7
Missing in action!

While I was happy for Polo and Monk for having been so courageous and getting the praise they richly deserved, I couldn't hide my sorrow and slowly slipped away with my heart sinking to my paws. I went slowly as if in a dream and sat on Monk's back steps wondering how I would cope if anything happened to Fromage. Cara came and sat beside me without saying a word and gently started licking my face. I guess she sensed my distress. Then Monk and Polo were also sitting beside me, not saying a word as if they believed that their very presence would give me strength. Strangely enough, it did. We sat like this, the four of us without moving or saying a word, I don't know for how long.

All at once, the silent night exploded into loud barks and Polo jerked his head saying, "That's Terrance." Polo and Monk ran through the cat flap to the front door like two consecutive bullets from a pistol while Cara and I stayed in the same position not daring to breath, out of concern on what news would follow.

Suddenly, they were all on me and Terrance came bounding up to us and said, "Gals, you can relax. We found Fromage. He is alright if somewhat rattled. Missy has taken him home to give him some warm milk and put him to bed. Solo told her that both of you were probably with Monk and that she should not worry about you. But I think it is best that you too go home. We can talk tomorrow."

I gave a loud sigh of relief. I felt the weight of the world that had descended on me quickly lift off my shoulders. I could easily have burst into tears just like Cara. But I didn't wish Cara to be distressed on my account nor Monk, Terrance and Polo. So I simply took a deep breath and for once even I was happy to let Cara take the lead and follow her back home. We were both anxious to get back to Missy and Fromage. We both wanted to check out Fromage and lick him and welcome him back home.

When we got to the cottage, Missy had already run a hot bath and given Fromage a good soaking. He had been very dirty and sniffy when they found him, but we did not want to ask questions as he had been given a good shampooing and blow dry followed by a towel rub; he had also drunk his hot milk and was settled down in his cot with Missy rubbing him gently to sleep. We went up to him and licked him *'welcome back'* and he gave us a drowsy lick in return and went back to sleep. I suspected Missy had given him some calming medicine recommended by our French vet to make him sleepy and calm down. She did this on exceptional occasions such as when we crossed over to London via the Channel, thinking the disruption was too much for us. I guess she thought that the experience of getting thrown out and finding himself alone on the streets of London was just too much excitement for even Fromage with his usual *'ce je ne sais quoi'* attitude towards life. Charlotte was all agog, her little nose twitching up and down nonstop. I said, "Don't worry, Charlotte – I will explain all in the morning. Don't be concerned, everything is just fine."

The events of that night were too much even for me. I decided to cuddle in bed with Missy and Cara that night, thinking how lucky we were to find good friends such as Terrance, Monk, Solo and Hobbs.

Solo had agreed to assist Missy without batting an eyelid or posing any questions or reflection. He and Monk had also done their job in catching the real culprit for the *Señora*. We would get the details the next day. I wanted to know where Fromage had been. Also, what had happened to Banks? Surely Monk and Terrance would know as they would have heard Inspector Reid and Solo talking. I wondered as I drifted to sleep what time the news would be broken to the *Señora*. Poor *Señora*! She would have to find a new major dome. But I am sure she would be happy to retrieve her diamond necklace and definitely not want to have a thief living in her house. Polo would be relieved too as I know that he never really liked Banks.

The next day Missy went to the shop as usual. But she did not wish to take Fromage with her as she thought that we all needed to catch up on our sleep and recover from the excitement of the previous night. So we had our breakfast and lounged about in our sunny kitchen.

Terrance, Polo and Monk came to see us around 11am. This was the first time they had visited since we moved in, but all three were familiar with the cottage having visited often when Aunt Florence was living there. Monk and Polo came in through the flap in the door and Monk very cleverly jumped up and opened the door for Terrance who was too big to crawl in through our flap door.

Terrance said to Fromage, "Not bedraggled any more, my lad? No broken bones, no wounds or scratches?" And as Fromage shook his head bashfully, Terrance said, "That's a relief, you gave us all a bit of a scare."

Fromage had bounced back very fast and had promised to tell Charlotte all that had happened that night. I had to smile though when he started explaining the difference in the texture between the French and English cheese as that is what had stuck foremost in his head.

Monk looked around and said that the cottage is even nicer than when Aunt Florence lived here. Cara and I beamed at him. I think he guessed that we are two house proud kitties. Our Fromage, being the little blabber mouth that he is, must have told all of them how finicky Missy was about keeping the house neat and clean and how Cara and I tended to take after Missy in this respect and enjoyed when the cottage was being made clean and beautiful. *C'est la vie!* That is how we are and we have no intention of hiding our positive characters.

We sat in the back porch overlooking our miniature back garden which was filled with shrubs and fragrant flowers with the summer sun shining on our backs. Monk filled us in on what had happened the previous night. Banks had been caught red handed. He had the diamond necklace in his bag hidden this time in a loaf of bread.

"Pas très originale, non?" I said to the others. Solo and Inspector Reid were wiser about the way Banks operated after Missy had revealed how Banks had hidden the necklace inside the cheese.

Banks had been handcuffed and led to the police car to be booked at the local police station. He would soon be in jail. Inspector Reid and Solo had waited until 10am the next morning to call on the *Señora* and break the news to her. She had been astonished to know that her necklace had been sitting inside the cheese all that time.

She had gathered Polo in her arms and said, "I knew my brave little Polo would not have allowed anyone to steal my necklace if he was awake." Inspector Reid had patted Polo on the head and said that he was a brave little dog and would certainly have taken action if he was awake. The *Señora* had said, "How dare Banks give a sleeping pill to Polo without consulting a vet, he could have really harmed Polo."

Polo was, of course, over the moon with the praise given by everyone. His eyes were shining as he recounted how they said that he was a brave little dog. I could visibly see him growing taller in stature. He really is a loyal and lovable Pekinese. Terrance and Monk had been right about that.

Solo had taken the *Señora's* necklace back to her and asked Hobbs to take her to the bank with it for safekeeping. Hobbs had taken her and Polo to the bank that morning to return the necklace to her vault.

I said to the gathered group, "Before we go any further, I would like to make a few remarks." It was my intention, as the eldest in the group, to thank Monk and Terrance on behalf of my family. I cleared my throat, ignoring the looks of amusement from Monk and Terrance, and was surprised that I was too choked up to say a word. It was only then that I recognized how worried I had been – filled with dread at the thought of losing our Fromage. I did not even admit it to myself until I saw my loved ones gathered around me. Cara, smiled tenderly at me, her lovely blue eyes filled with love; Charlotte eyed me with adoration, her little nose twitching with excitement; Fromage smiled encouragingly at me full of admiration, and yes, even Monk and Terrance were looking at me with respect and affection.

They were all waiting for me to speak but Monk realized that my emotions were making me speechless and said, "I trust the sermon will not be too long, Inca," with an encouraging smile.

With everyone's peal of laughter, my voice jumped back into my throat and I said, "On behalf of Missy and her family, I wish to thank Solo and his troupe from the bottom of our hearts for helping us to find Fromage. We cherish and appreciate your friendship and also you, Polo, who have conducted yourself admirably in the face of difficult circumstances, and we are eternally in your debt."

Charlotte contributed with, "Well said, Inca."

I asked Monk if Solo had explained how the robbery took place. Yes, fairly simply apparently. Before taking the *Señora* to her lawyer, Banks had prepared a nice meal for Polo. What Polo did not know was that Banks had crushed a sleeping tablet into the food. Polo had been fast asleep when an accomplice had entered through the back door conveniently left open by Banks.

The accomplice had walked upstairs and pinched the necklace. Banks had bought this large cheese and the accomplice had placed it in the middle where Banks had already dug a hole. The necklace was then covered with the cheese that had been dug out. The accomplice had slipped out the same way she had come, leaving the back door widely open. The whole operation had taken less than 10 minutes

When Banks and the *Señora* came back, Polo had just woken up and had been rather groggy, but, in the excitement of discovering the theft of the diamond necklace, the arrival of the police and the hue and cry thereafter, nobody had noticed little Polo's yawns.

Banks admitted all this at the police station and even gave up his accomplice, who turned out to be the manicurist of the *Señora* - Polly. This manicurist visited several wealthy homes in the area, including the *Señora*, and even if she was seen around the neighborhood, no one would have thought anything of it. Banks had been crafty in befriending Polly. I wondered how many more homes Banks would have raided secretly after selling the *Señora's* diamond necklace together with Polly. They would have formed a formidable team if they had not been foiled.

Banks, despite his huge size, was a coward after all and had started blabbing everything to the police when he got caught red handed. The question on everyone's lips was why did the accomplice not take away the diamond necklace but leave it in the house. This, according to Banks, was because he did not trust anyone else to keep the necklace. He wanted it kept under his watchful eye. No one had suspected that the necklace was hidden in the innocent cheese ball visible to anyone who passed the pantry. Banks had not reckoned with Fromage and his passion for cheese.

The police had not suspected that the necklace was in the middle of the cheese. Solo had suspected that Banks had something to do with the theft, but, since he was in the city with the *Señora* the whole time, he had an airtight alibi. The necklace had also disappeared. Hobbs had gone around the usual known jewelry fencers, but nothing had appeared in the market.

Banks had confessed that he wished to continue to work for the *Señora* for another year or so before quietly resigning from his post and leaving the country with the necklace to dispose of it outside of the UK.

Fromage recounted his story of when he fell with the cheese having dug out the necklace. "I was so surprised that I could not move. Just as Jacques had once saved me, I thought Banks picked me up out of kindness to ensure that I had not hurt myself with the necklace entangled around my body. Imagine my surprise when he ran to the front door and threw me out. It is then that I let out a surprised yell. I had never been outside of the street before. I was not hurt though and I had yelled out in surprise. I landed on my four feet; the fall was not that long. But I was confused when I recovered, about where I should go as there was no visible entrance to the cottage from this side of the street. I noticed the large garage door of the *Señora's* house but it was closed so I had no way of getting back in. Across the street which was well lit, I noticed a large park fenced in, but it was so dark that I had reservations about going there. I just ran further down the street and sat in the doorway of the house I knew was Monk's. I could smell Terrance on the steps so I knew it was the correct house. I was relieved thinking that Terrance would come out with Hobbs around 6am.

"But I suddenly recalled Polo's and Monk's warning about Boss. My fear was that Boss, the Rottweiler that Terrance had asked us to watch out for, would take his morning walk before Terrance." Reading Fromage's mind, I saw that all the bravery had fled from him with the possibility of actually having to face Boss by himself. It would have been foolish in any case for him to have tried to deal with Boss by himself and I was thankful that he had the sense to hide from Boss.

I licked him and said, "You were very correct, Fromage" and Cara added, "I would have done the same."

He looked at us sheepishly and decided to come clean. "You cannot imagine the fear that entered my mind thinking of an encounter with Boss," continued Fromage. "I thought I should be brave like Monk and face up to him. To be honest, I don't think I could have done that. So I decided to hide in the park in case Boss came out for his walk before Terrance. I crossed the street, jumped on the wall to climb down on the other side. But my foot slipped and I landed in this huge rubbish patch of leaves and manure. It was a soft landing though so I did not hurt myself but I knew I did not have pleasant smell. I didn't mind the smell but knew for certain the gals would object vehemently. However, I couldn't do anything about it."

"Then I realized that Inca and Monk would have been in Polo's house and Cara had witnessed the whole episode from under the table and would have alerted Inca of what happened. I tried to console myself that someone would come looking for me soon."

Terrance said, "It was not too difficult for me to locate Fromage as we found his little beret outside the house of the *Señora*. Missy saw it and recognized it instantly. It must have slipped off when he

152

was thrown out. Solo held it to my nose and said, *'Sniff, Terrance, sniff! Go, good boy, find Fromage'.*"

"I could get his smell up to the point where he must have leaped up the wall. So I sat in that spot and looked at Solo and up to the wall. Solo is pretty smart at reading my gestures and guessed that Fromage had climbed over the wall at that spot. So we went into Kensington Gardens from the little gate at the end of the street. At that time of the night, the garden was closed. Solo managed to open the gate by using one of the several keys he kept on himself. Solo is a dapper hand at opening other people's doors."

"From that point it was not too difficult; Solo led us to the point where I had sat down on the other side. I soon got the scent of Fromage once again and found him on this patch of manure looking very dirty and sorry for himself indeed."

Fromage said, "You cannot imagine my relief in hearing Missy's voice and being taken in her arms despite my dirty condition. She just ignored the dirt I was covered in."

I said, "You probably don't realize the relief Missy must have felt finding you. She was so worried about you that she was in tears as was little Cara. You really worried us, Fromage, even though your action in the pantry helped in pointing the finger at Banks as the real culprit and taking the shadow of doubt that had lain on poor *Señora*." Fromage came up to me and licked my face and that of Cara.

He then nuzzled Charlotte who in return snuggled into his scarf and said, "*Mon Ami*, what a terrible experience. I should have been with you." Fromage said, "next time you will, Charlotte."
I frowned, "Next time, Fromage? There will be no next time. Please get that in to your head."

Monk smiled and said, "All's well that ends well."

I had to admit it was a relief. It was good to have all of us safe and sound at home and listen to another story from Terrance that made us forget the terrible night.

The next morning the argument started out of thin air.

Missy wished to talk to Aunt Florence before she and Fromage went off to the shop for the morning. When Missy had her weekly conversation with Aunt Florence we knew it usually took quite some time as she had a habit of recounting every little detail of what she did the previous week, all the plans that were bubbling in her head for the expansion of the business, and a host of other important and not so important matters pertaining to our lives.

Today's conversation was going to be an especially long one as she wished to inform Aunt Florence all about the *Senora*'s diamond necklace. All the tiny details would be divulged, from when it was stolen to it being found, and Fromage's role in the whole story, not to mention meeting Solo and Hobbs. Solo's kindness in helping her to find our Fromage when he went missing on the streets of London was to be the highlight of the conversation today.

Leaving the others playing in the kitchen, I accompanied Missy to have the Skype conversation with Aunt Florence. I loved it when, on seeing me on the screen, she went into rhapsodies in her lilting sweet voice calling me '*ma Cherie*'. Needless to say, Aunt Florence is one of my most ardent admirers. After the initial greetings when she gently cooed to me, I gave her one of my special looks from my dreamy eyes and she fussed over me some more. I then left Missy to get on with the rest of her conversation and went to see what the others were doing downstairs, hoping that they hadn't finished off the croquettes in the tray we jointly shared.

I tripped down the stairs, light as a feather, thinking happily to myself, '*Another deliciously hot summer morning, I need to make the most of it by sunbathing on Monks' warm green lawn*'.

I had heard that the weather in London tended to lean towards rain and drizzle and once the showers kicked in, it would continue to do so indefinitely, as London is famous for its wet weather. I was thinking to myself, '*How lucky it was that we came to London in the summer time so that we could enjoy the outdoors before being housebound due to nasty weather*'. We had heard Missy discussing the terrible weather in London with Genevieve. She had said that it usually rains cats and dogs. That had given us something to think about and Charlotte had mischievously punned, "Missy would need an umbrella made of steel to keep off all the Polos and Incas falling from the sky."

"Ha-ha very funny, Charlotte," I had retorted.

At the bottom of the stairs, I practiced a salsa move humming to myself *'Olé! Olé!'* – quick step then hind legs to the right and head to the left, *'Olé! Olé!'* – another quick step then hind legs to the left and head to the right *'Olé! Olé!'* I truly enjoyed my supple salsa moves. Since no one was around, my usual serious countenance for once reaped into a deep smile like the Cheshire cat that we had watched with Missy on the screen from the Disney animated film, *Alice in Wonderland.* I wondered if I should teach Monk some salsa moves. I had noticed that he was pretty nimble on his paws, despite his rotund waist line. *'Hmmm... perhaps he could salsa with me'.*

Tossing the last *'Olé! Olé!'* in the air, I entered the kitchen looking forward to my snack and a yarn with the gang when I stopped short. The atmosphere in the kitchen was glacial and I felt as if someone had thrown a bowl of cold water in my face. Cara was sitting as if she had swallowed a pincushion and Fromage had a terrible scowl on his face. Charlotte had her back to him with her arms crossed quivering with rage.

"What on earth is going on here?" I asked. "After yesterday's tender and happy reunion, how did things go sour so fast? Why is everyone looking so mad?"

There was a long silence and then all three of them started babbling at the same time.

Charlotte said, "I am never going to talk to Fromage again," with Fromage quipping, "It is entirely the fault of Charlotte. I told her not to go out of the house to see anyone when we were not around. Charlotte should obey me."
Obey him? Has Fromage entered the dark ages?' I thought to myself. *'What is he talking about? Where was our good natured and happy-go-lucky Fromage?'*

"Silence," I exploded. I looked at Cara and said, "What is going on, Cara? It was just a few minutes ago when everything was going well. What happened when I left the kitchen?"

Cara whispered to me, "Fromage was terribly mean to Charlotte. She was telling us how Polo and she went for a walk in his garden and Fromage threw a fit. I have never seen him so nasty to Charlotte before. He actually hissed and bared his fangs at her."

Understanding hit me. My eyes narrowed - I remember the scene when I had observed Fromage's jealous fit when he noticed Polo's sudden liking for Charlotte and the mean comments he had been making to her when we got interrupted by the Banks episode. I said, "Fromage, let's go somewhere private, I need to have a word with you."

Just then Missy came running down the stairs, saying, "Let's go, Fromage." She swooped him in her arms and raced to her bicycle, throwing us a kiss. They hurried off; Missy riding the bicycle with Fromage in the basket.

My private conversation with Fromage would have to wait. Thinking nothing more of it and hoping Charlotte would cool down soon enough, I looked at Cara and Charlotte and said, "Why don't the two you play together while I take a nap?" and trotted off to my comfy cot to have a cat nap.

I was woken up from a pleasant dream where I was sitting having a deep conversation with my hero, Dr. House, as he was congratulating me for my quick thinking in helping him solve his most difficult case, when I heard Missy's bicycle turning into the cottage. I found Cara snoozing next to me, and gently nudged her to wake up. I raced downstairs to welcome them at the door, while a sleepy Cara followed me, shaking her head awake.

Fromage had a marvelously busy day at the store and wanted to tell us all about it while Missy was fixing herself a sandwich. Missy carried her sandwich upstairs to work on her plan to expand the store's business.

"Where is Charlotte?" asked Fromage, getting all ready to relate what he did at the store. He preferred to have his audience lined up like soldiers in a parade before he started. His tales tend to be rather long and detailed though, I must admit, interesting. We usually listened, with Charlotte asking most of the questions which only made these stories even longer.

I looked around but couldn't see her. "Perhaps she is in the attic," I said and asked Cara to go upstairs while I took a look around our private garden as I knew that Charlotte liked to scuttle around, examining the bushes and plants and sniffing the air. However, Charlotte was not to be found in the attic, in the bedroom or in the garden.

Cara said, "I tried to interest Charlotte in a game after you went to take a nap, Inca, but she was so disheartened that she wanted to be left alone. I left her then and came upstairs to take a nap with you."

"Charlotte has run away? Oh no! This is your doing, Fromage," I said. "We need to have a long and serious conversation about how you have been treating Charlotte."

Fromage hung his head. "I am sorry, Inca," he said. "I promise I will never be mean to her again. But she is also to blame as she doesn't listen to me anymore." I sighed.

"This is not true, Fromage. Charlotte is a loyal friend. She is also an independent free spirit; you cannot behave as if she cannot have any other friends besides us. You know that you do spend a lot of time with Monk since we came to London, and neither Charlotte nor we have ever objected to this."

"But Monk is a cat like me," he moaned. I frowned with annoyance; Fromage was giving true meaning to the saying 'like a jealous cat'.

I was about to comment on the absurdness of this statement when I heard a small faint sound from outside. "It sounds as if someone is in trouble," I said. The sound came again and we rushed outside to see where it came from.

Monk and Terrance had heard the noise as well and had come out in a rush to see where it was coming from. The sound came again, and there was no doubt about it; the sound was of someone frightened and in pain – and young, judging by the pitch of its voice.

The sound had come from the side of the house where Hobbs had some work going on above the garage roof. We all looked up and we saw Charlotte high above us perched on the ledge of the high ceiling of Monk's enormous house.

Terrance gasped, "How on earth did she get up there? It looks as if she has hurt herself and is unable to get down."

Fromage gasped, "I am going up, Inca. I have to get her down."

"Fromage," I hurriedly ordered him. "No, you cannot, I will go up." We all know that Fromage is not sure footed at all. He has the tendency to fall off a three feet high bench and I know that Cara is timid of heights, even if she doesn't like to show it.

Monk gallantly said, "No let me go up."

I said to Monk, "No, Monk. It is kind of you, but please let me go. The rooftop looks fragile since the work has not been completed. Your weight may bring down the lose tiles."

So saying, I removed my shawl and tossed it to Cara for safekeeping and quickly hoisted myself up onto the gnarled old tree trunk that provided nooks for my sharp claws and climbing space in its thick curving branches which grew alongside the house reaching up to the roof. I have always been agile as a monkey. With my heart beating with concern for Charlotte who seemed to be in pain from the tone of her voice, I climbed the tree as rapidly as I could while pulling myself from one branch to another. My strong sturdy forelegs served me well. There was a long narrow branch almost touching the roof. I took this route balancing on the slender space and climbed onto the precarious roof that was being retiled by Hobbs. Charlotte must have come this way, I thought.

I guessed that Hobbs had taken a break for lunch and would be back to complete the work. The ledge where Charlotte was lying was not easily accessible and I had to cross a roof that was being repaired which did not look very secure. Charlotte was very frightened indeed and tried to reach me. Her scrambling movement only served to loosen more of the slippery tiles which tumbled down to the floor.

Trying not to show Charlotte how anxious I was, I said, "Charlotte, don't move, please, stay still, I will get to you." I started gently purring to lull her fears. I whispered, "Are you hurt badly, Charlotte?"

She whispered back, "One of my paws is hurt, Inca. I don't seem to be able run as before." My heart skipped a beat, has she broken her little leg?

"I will soon get you down and Missy will take care of you," I said as confidently as I could.

Instead of trying to get to her directly, I went slowly past her on the good side of the roof and climbed higher than her, clutching onto a tile that was firmly fixed with my sharp long claws. I then gently let my long thick tail hang in front of Charlotte and asked her, "Do you think you could hang on to my tail, Charlotte? Your front paws are not hurt, are they?"

She replied in a quivering voice, "My front paws are not hurting, Inca."

"Not to worry, I will soon get you down and Missy will take care of your leg," I said again, letting my thick furry tail swing down right in front of her. She clutched on to my tail, and when I felt her little paws firmly hanging on to my tail, I slowly started moving back to the narrow branch.

Our progress was slow as I did not wish to miss my step. Every now and then I stopped to encourage Charlotte to keep a firm grip of my tail. I looked down once to see the anxious upturned faces of my comrades. I heard Monk urge me not to look down but to keep going, adding, "You can do it, Inca. Brave girl, keep moving." This was the tricky bit, as the branch was very narrow, whispering to Charlotte once again to hang on and not let go at all costs, I started placing one paw after another firmly on the narrow space, humming to myself to get my thoughts away from the steepness of the drop and what would happen to Charlotte if I missed my step.

As I reached the end of the branch, Monk was there to help me. He knew this tree very well as he had climbed it numerous times. He also seemed to sense that it would be harder for me to come down rather than going up. He asked Charlotte to climb on to his neck and, together with Charlotte, we carefully came down the trunk all the way to the solid ground.

Everyone on the ground gave a collective sigh of relief, while Terrance said, "A brave rescue effort, Inca and Monk, you make a good team."

I could see panic in Fromage's eyes, despite his monotonous muttering. He said, "Put her down, Monk. Charlotte tightened her grip around Monk's neck and with a cheeky grin said, "Not while he is so angry." So Charlotte was her normal spirited self, in spite of her wounded leg.

"You two, enough of this nonsense," I said in an exasperated voice. "First of all, I am taking Charlotte to Missy to have a look at her foot and then young Fromage, I need to have a serious talk with you privately." After saying that, I left them behind to discuss what happened. I transferred Charlotte to my neck and, thanking Monk hurriedly, I rushed Charlotte to the cottage and up to Missy. Fromage followed me and I knew that, despite the tantrums, he was greatly concerned that Charlotte was in pain. Charlotte is important and precious to him, and she will always be.

Missy examined Charlotte's leg which she then neatly splintered, saying, "Charlotte, no more running about for you for a few weeks until your leg is nicely healed." Missy being Missy, called up the neighborhood vet to make an emergency appointment to check on Charlotte's leg to be sure that there was no permanent damage. Naturally, Fromage wanted to go too, and so did we. Missy called the vet back and explained that we had just arrived from Paris and asked if she could bring all of us over to have us registered at the clinic. So we all got into Missy's hatchback and away we went.

Dr. Abigail Bristow, the vet, greeted us at the clinic. She had a cheerful and agreeable disposition and laughter rather like a small firecracker going off. She seemed just the opposite of our vet in Paris. Dr. Bristow was shaped like a large German sausage, very tight around the middle and very full above and below with warm honey colored eyes. She hummed over us like a large bumble bee and gently petted Charlotte, saying, "We will soon take care of you, sweetheart." The leg had not been broken, just sprained and Dr. Bristol promised that Charlotte would soon be back on her feet.

Since we were to be Dr. Bristol's new clients, she had a look at each of us, laughing and talking all the time. Still remembering our experience with our Paris vet, we stood still while she gently felt us and examined our eyes, etc. "Excellent, excellent," she said. "Don't hesitate to call me, should you ever need any advice or have a problem," she reassured Missy.

Before too long we were back at home with Charlotte's leg neatly bandaged. We all made a great fuss of Charlotte and she seemed to have forgotten her pain with all the attention she was receiving. I had a serious conversation with Fromage soon after. The thought of Charlotte getting hurt seemed to have brought him to his senses.

In all modesty, I had the situation under control in 15 minutes flat. We were all back to normal, Fromage with his beret firmly in place and Charlotte her little neckerchief adjusted by Cara. In my opinion, Charlotte needed rest and nourishment to make a full recovery. Fromage refused to leave her side despite my argument that she should rest. He apologized profusely to Charlotte and promised never to say anything mean to her ever again.

Charlotte smiled happily and said, "I am sorry too and will never run away again either. Let's go together to see Polo, how about that, *Mon Ami?*"

Fromage agreed quickly. At that moment, Charlotte's wish was his command. Charlotte continued with a smile, "Inca, I owe my life to you twice over now."

Taking a leaf from Aunt Florence, I just smiled at her and said, "For you, *ma Chérie*, any time." Honestly, Charlotte is a little sweetheart. Despite her wounded leg, she was back to being her cheerful and thoughtful self.

Charlotte, she is a sweetheart!

Chapter 8
All is purrrfect!

We were all seated outside on the lawn of Solo's garden. There was a long trestle table on which an ivory cloth had been laid out by Hobbs to spread a feast of both French and English cuisines. There were plenty of French cheeses with fresh baguettes, succulent roast beef prepared by Hobbs and an enormous sugar-cured ham bought from the famous Harrods that Terrance always speaks of. Other types of little tarts both sweet and savory prepared by Genevieve and French wines from the shop were also laid out. In addition, the table was loaded with goodies prepared by Polo's Mrs. Applebee, the *Señora*'s contribution to the picnic.

Hobbs had very quickly found a kindly middle-aged couple, relatives of his, to look after the *Señora* with the abrupt but welcome departure of Banks, at least on the side of the animal domain. They were a couple named Mr. and Mrs. Applebee. Mrs. Applebee was round, cherubic and cheerful, while Mr. Applebee a was tall, thin and dignified man who rarely spoke. She would cook and he would drive and tend to the large garden and act as chief servant. They both liked dogs and Polo took an instant liking to them. Polo told us that he was sure they would look after his *Señora* well. Terrance vouched for the couple saying, "Any relative of Hobbs gets full marks from me."

Mr. and Mrs. Applebee had attacked the house and were still at it, cleaning it from top to bottom. Because the *Señora*, since she heard of the disappearance of her husband, had never come out of her room other than in the night to roam around the corridors upstairs, had never noticed nor cared how Banks was neglecting the house. Mrs. Applebee had said the house was going to the dogs! Polo said he couldn't understand what she meant by that. In any

163

case, every nook and cranny of the large, well-designed house was constantly being dusted, vacuumed and washed. Polo usually turned up at our place or that of Monk when Mrs. Applebee was on the warpath with her duster, vacuum cleaner and polish. Polo told us that he preferred to stay away until all the pounding, dusting and vacuuming was over. In his words, *'I need a bit of peace'*.

There had been several visits between Missy and the *Señora*. Missy's furry friends had also visited the *Señora* often and I had made it a point to cuddle up to her and gaze into her eyes, conveying constant messages of love and friendship. True to her promise, she had started walking every morning with Polo on his leash. They often bumped into Boss, but Polo, himself confident in the arm of his famous *Señora*, just walked by Boss and his sweaty pack leader with his little pug nose in the air. As he remarked to us, "Who cares or has time for unpleasant dogs with their not so pleasant smelling pack leaders when I have my beloved and renowned mistress by my side?"

One fine early morning, Missy had met the *Señora* at the Kensington Gardens and invited her for a cup of tea and croissants. The lady enjoyed herself so much that this became a daily habit. How could she not? Missy is a friendly and caring chatterbox, and we were all at home, including Charlotte that she had not met before - happy to have her as our guest. She was delighted to visit the cottage as she used to when Aunt Florence was living there.

While Missy was serving tea to the *Señora* one morning, just to show off and get some attention, I admit, I proudly gave a performance of my salsa dancing capability to the rhythm and beat of the Latin music that I love. She was so amazed! She said, "*Estupenda mi* Inca!" She even joined me, swaying gently to the Latin music with sudden spirals and turns like an old pro. The others watched admiringly and Missy clapped her hands with glee.

Solo and the Inspector had also become friends with Missy and the *Señora*. Solo had always been chummy with Raoul and known the *Senora*. But when Raoul went missing, the *Señora* had withdrawn not wanting to meet anyone who reminded her of her dear loving husband. Solo, sensitive to her feelings, had left her in peace, but felt he had left her too long to wallow in her sadness. In any case, she seemed to be coming out of her shell. He had invited the *Señora* and Missy for dinner several evenings and, of course, we went along with Missy uninvited. It had been very pleasant listening to jazz music and enjoying Hobbs's good food while the furry friends enjoyed each other's company and that of our human companions. Hobbs never forgets us and there was always an extra plate of delicious food beside Monk's and Terrance's plates.

At one of those dinners, Solo asked the *Señora* if she would like to join him on one of his quests for fundraising for the rescue home that he had introduced to Raoul. Yes, it turned out that it was with Solo that the *Señora*'s husband had first visited the rescue home and seen Polo and thought he would make a good gift for his beloved wife. After that, together with Solo, Raoul had been a kind benefactor to the rescue home.

Reluctantly at first, the *Señora* had agreed and then become passionate about its cause after visiting the home and meeting the animals longing to be adopted by a kind family. She put all her connections to this cause and was dedicated to the success of the rescue home and its inmates. So, with going for daily morning walks, having breakfast with us and being occupied with the well-being of the rescue home, she had her hands full. Although she never stopped thinking of her beloved husband, she had so much more to occupy herself that she had slowly started accepting invitations to concerts and functions where she always campaigned for the rescue home. She had slowly reverted back to her normal self. The grungy, shapeless clothes were gradually abandoned and she started getting back to her enticing exotic wardrobe.

More interestingly, following the recovery of the costly diamond necklace, the insurance company had paid a visit to the *Señora*. There was a reward for those who were responsible for recovering the necklace. The necklace was truly very valuable, valued at nearly half a million pounds. Imagine that! After a long discussion, Missy, Solo and the *Señora* decided to give the reward from the insurance company to Polo's *alma mater* – the rescue home. The inmates of the rescue home needed this gift far more than any of us.

It was a wonderful hot summer day. The sun was shining and my doggy friends were romping around in the garden playing catch with Hobbs. I had never seen little Polo looking so carefree and happy. He kept running after Terrance and then running up to the *Señora* to lick her hand, panting away with a wide open grin with his pink tongue hanging out.

The spat between Fromage and Charlotte had soon cleared up. They went together each Sunday afternoon to see Polo and take a walk around his garden. Fromage now had two ardent listeners to the happenings in his cheese shop.

Monk and I were sitting on the hot step leading from the main house to the garden, enjoying the sun. Solo's large garden was at its best. Our own cottage hidden at the bottom of the garden looked like a large friendly, white, curled up octopus wearing a large thatched black beret. The sky matched the color of Cara's blue eyes while the foliage competed with Monk's eyes – sparkling green and gold.

Cara and Fromage were trying out their tree climbing skills on the oak tree in the garden imitating me the day I ran up the tree to rescue Charlotte. As to be expected, Fromage kept tumbling off and quickly looking around to see if anyone noticed; he pretended to be cool about the fall and licked his tail vigorously before climbing the tree again.

The *Señora* was sitting gracefully on a garden chair with big sunglasses and an even bigger sun hat to protect her from the sun. She looked happy and content and was listening to Missy and Jacques's conversation about the new shop with an easy smile. Inspector Reid had lost his sad and dull expression; he was laughing and talking with the group, offering Missy and Jacques advice on our café shop. Solo was sitting on his chair with his head back, enjoying the sun on his face. Soft jazz music seeped out of the house. Little Charlotte was sitting under a shady umbrella in her small cage munching on a sliver of cheese. She was back to normal, but Missy was still anxious about her leg. To ensure that Charlotte did not miss the fun, Missy kept her in the shade in her cage under the umbrella.

Monk and I on the stairs leading to his garden

Hobbs was serving cocktails and Genevieve was passing her freshly baked tarts around nonstop.

"What an adventure we have had!" I said to Monk. "Thank you for including us. Who would have thought three cats that have been living a peaceful life in Paris would be engrossed in such an escapade?"

"Peaceful life!" retorted Monk. "I heard about your last escapade to say *adios* to your Cat Council before leaving Paris from Fromage. I wish I get the chance to visit Paris one day. By the way, one of these days I will introduce you to the Cat Council of Kensington."

"Nevertheless, you are most welcome," added Monk with a smile. "It has been a pleasure meeting you and your family. I am glad Missy decided to stay on in London for now. Hopefully, Missy's gals and Fromage will be able to assist Solo and company to solve more such mysteries in the future."

I smiled back at him demurely, but said to myself, *'Next time, Mon Ami, it will be I who will catch the villain, c'est moi, pas toi!'*.

I breathed in the fresh air and looked at the blue skies shining above our heads, my little sister and brother enjoying climbing up their first tree trunk while Charlotte enjoyed everyone's company.

Missy's golden streaks sparkled in the sun and her happy laughter tinkled in the wind and I said to myself, *'There is always a next time for more new adventures for the famous Dr. House, the pussy cat version... but for the moment, life is purrfect!'*

My troupe and I, hasta la vista, baby!

Translations

French	English
C'est la vie	*That's life*
Ce je ne sais quoi	*A pleasant quality that is hard to describe*
Chéri (m), Chérie (f)	*Darling*
Excusez-moi	*Excuse me*
Fromage	*Cheese*
Jamais de la vie !	*Not on your life*
Les huit familles de fromage	*The eight families of cheese*
Ma Chérie (f)	*My dear*
Moi Me C'est moi, pas toi !	*It is me not you*
Mon Dieu!	*My goodness*
Pain complet	*Whole-wheat bread*
Pas très *original*	*Not very original*
Pourquoi pas ?	*Why not ?*
Très chic, non?	*Very stylish, no?*
Quel Bonheur!	*What happiness!*
Quoi?	*What?*

Spanish	English
Adios	*Goodbye*
Estupenda mi Inca!	*Wonderful my Inca!*
Ay, Caramba!	*An expression denoting surprise*

CPSIA information can be obtained
at www.ICGtesting.com
Printed in the USA
BVHW041816081219
566035BV00006B/215/P